MagicHigh School

YOTSUBA SUCCESSION ARC

16

Tsutomu Sato

Illustration Kana Ishida

YEN ON

NEW YORK

THE IRREGULAR AT MAGIC HIGH SCHOOL
TSUTOMU SATO

Translation by Andrew Prowse
Cover art by Kana Ishida

This book is a work of fiction. Names, characters, places, and incidents are the product of the author's imagination or are used fictitiously. Any resemblance to actual events, locales, or persons, living or dead, is coincidental.

MAHOUKA KOUKOU NO RETTOUSEI Vol. 16
©TSUTOMU SATO 2015
First published in Japan in 2015 by KADOKAWA CORPORATION, Tokyo.
English translation rights arranged with KADOKAWA CORPORATION, Tokyo, through Tuttle-Mori Agency, Inc., Tokyo.

English translation © 2021 by Yen Press, LLC

Yen On
150 West 30th Street, 19th Floor
New York, NY 10001

Visit us at yenpress.com
facebook.com/yenpress
twitter.com/yenpress
yenpress.tumblr.com
instagram.com/yenpress

First Yen On Edition: April 2021

Yen On is an imprint of Yen Press, LLC.
The Yen On name and logo are trademarks of Yen Press, LLC.

The publisher is not responsible for websites (or their content) that are not owned by the publisher.

Library of Congress Cataloging-in-Publication Data
Names: Satou, Tsutomu. | Ishida, Kana, illustrator.
Title: The irregular at Magic High School / Tsutomu Satou ; Illustrations by Kana Ishida.
Other titles: Mahōka kōkō no rettosei. English
Description: First Yen On edition. | New York, NY : Yen On, 2016—
Identifiers: LCCN 2015042401 | ISBN 9780316348805 (v 1 : pbk.) | ISBN 9780316390293 (v. 2 : pbk.) |
    ISBN 9780316390309 (v. 3 : pbk.) | ISBN 9780316390316 (v. 4 : pbk.) |
    ISBN 9780316390323 (v. 5 : pbk.) | ISBN 9780316390330 (v. 6 : pbk.) |
    ISBN 9781975300074 (v. 7 : pbk.) | ISBN 9781975327125 (v. 8 : pbk.) |
    ISBN 9781975327149 (v. 9 : pbk.) | ISBN 9781975327163 (v. 10 : pbk.) |
    ISBN 9781975327187 (v. 11 : pbk.) | ISBN 9781975327200 (v. 12 : pbk.) |
    ISBN 9781975332327 (v. 13 : pbk.) | ISBN 9781975332471 (v. 14 : pbk.) |
    ISBN 9781975332495 (v. 15 : pbk.) | ISBN 9781975332518 (v. 16 : pbk.)
Subjects: CYAC: Brothers and sisters—Fiction. | Magic—Fiction. | High schools—Fiction. |
    Schools—Fiction. | Japan—Fiction. | Science fiction.
Classification: LCC PZ7.1.S265 Ir 2016 | DDC [Fic]—dc23
LC record available at http://lccn.loc.gov/2015042401

ISBNs: 978-1-9753-3251-8 (paperback)
       978-1-9753-3252-5 (ebook)

10 9 8 7 6 5 4 3 2 1

LSC-C

Printed in the United States of America

The Irregular at Magic High School

YOTSUBA SUCCESSION ARC

An irregular older brother with a certain flaw.
An honor roll younger sister who is perfectly flawless.

When the two siblings enrolled in Magic High School,
a dramatic life unfolded—

Character

Tatsuya Shiba

Class 2-E. Advanced to the newly established magic engineering course. Approaches everything in a detached manner. His sister Miyuki's Guardian.

Miyuki Shiba

Class 2-A. Tatsuya's younger sister; enrolled as the top student last year. Specializes in freezing magic. Dotes on her older brother.

Leonhard Saijou

Class 2-F. Tatsuya's friend. Course 2 student. Specializes in hardening magic. Has a bright personality.

Erika Chiba

Class 2-F. Tatsuya's friend. Course 2 student. A charming troublemaker.

Mizuki Shibata

Class 2-E. In Tatsuya's class again this year. Has pushion radiation sensitivity. Serious and a bit of an airhead.

Mikihiko Yoshida

Class 2-B. This year he became a Course 1 student. From a famous family that uses ancient magic. Has known Erika since they were children.

Honoka Mitsui

Class 2-A. Miyuki's classmate. Specializes in light-wave vibration magic. Impulsive when emotional.

Shizuku Kitayama

Class 2-A. Miyuki's classmate. Specializes in vibration and acceleration magic. Doesn't show emotional ups and downs very much.

Subaru Satomi

Class 2-D. Frequently mistaken for a pretty boy. Cheerful and easy to get along with.

Eimi Akechi

Class 2-B. A quarter-blood. Full name is Amelia Eimi Akechi Goldie. Daughter of the notable Goldie family.

Akaha Sakurakouji

Class 2-B. Friends with Subaru and Amy. Wears gothic lolita clothes and loves theme parks.

Shun Morisaki

Class 2-A. Miyuki's classmate. Specializes in CAD quick-draw. Takes great pride in being a Course 1 student.

Hagane Tomitsuka

Class 2-E. A magic martial arts user with the nickname "Range Zero." Uses magic martial arts.

Mayumi Saegusa

An alum. College student at the Magic University. Has a devilish personality but weak when on the defensive.

Azusa Nakajou

A senior. Former student council president. Shy and has trouble expressing herself.

Suzune Ichihara

An alum. College student at the Magic University. Calm, collected, and book smart.

Hanzou Gyoubu-Shoujou Hattori

A senior. Former head of the club committee. Gifted but can be too serious at times.

Mari Watanabe

An alum. Mayumi's good friend. Well rounded and likes a sporting fight.

Katsuto Juumonji

An alum and former head of the club committee. Has advanced to Magic University. "A boulder-like person," according to Tatsuya.

Koutarou Tatsumi

An alum and former member of the disciplinary committee. Has a heroic and dynamic personality.

Midori Sawaki

A senior. Member of the disciplinary committee. Has a complex about his girlish name.

Isao Sekimoto

An alum and former member of the disciplinary committee. Lost the school election. Committed acts of spying.

Kei Isori

A senior. Former student council treasurer. Excels in magical theory. Engaged to Kanon.

Takeaki Kirihara

A senior. Member of the *kenjutsu* club. Junior High Kanto Kenjutsu Tournament champion.

Kanon Chiyoda

A senior. Former chairwoman of the disciplinary committee. As confrontational as her predecessor, Mari.

Sayaka Mibu

A senior. Member of the kendo club. Placed second in the nation at the girl's junior high kendo tournament.

Takuma Shippou

The head of this year's new students. Course 1. Eldest son of the Shippou, one of the Eighteen, families with excellent magicians.

Kasumi Saegusa

A new student who enrolled at Magic High School this year. Mayumi Saegusa's younger sister.

Minami Sakurai

A new student who enrolled at Magic High School this year. Presents herself as Tatsuya and Miyuki's cousin. A Guardian candidate for Miyuki.

Izumi Saegusa

A new student who enrolled at Magic High School this year. Mayumi Saegusa's younger sister. Kasumi's younger twin sister. Meek and gentle personality.

Kento Smith

Class 1-G. A Caucasian boy whose parents are naturalized Japanese citizens from the USNA.

Koharu Hirakawa

An alum and engineer during the Nine School Competition last year. Withdrew from the Thesis Competition.

Chiaki Hirakawa

Class 2-E. Holds enmity toward Tatsuya.

Tomoko Chikura

A senior. Competitor in the women's solo Shields Down, a Nine School Competition event.

Tsugumi Igarashi

An alum.
Former biathlon club president.

Yousuke Igarashi

A junior. Tsugumi's younger brother. Has a somewhat reserved personality.

Kerry Minakami

A senior. Male representative for the main Monolith Code event at the Nine School Competition.

Satomi Asuka

First High nurse. Gentle, calm, and warm. Smile popular among male students.

Kazuo Tsuzura

First High teacher. Main field is magic geometry. Manager of the Thesis Competition team.

Jennifer Smith

A Caucasian naturalized as a Japanese citizen. Instructor for Tatsuya's class and for magic engineering classes.

Haruka Ono

A general counselor of First High. Tends to get bullied but has another side to her personality.

Yakumo Kokonoe

A user of an ancient magic called *ninjutsu*. Tatsuya's martial arts master.

Pixie

A home helper robot belonging to Magic High School. Official name 3H (Humanoid Home Helper: a human-shaped chore-assisting robot) Type P94.

Masaki Ichijou

A junior at Third High. Participating in the Nine School Competition this year as well. Direct heir to the Ichijou family, one of the Ten Master Clans.

Shinkurou Kichijouji

A junior at Third High. Participating in the Nine School Competition this year as well. Also known as Cardinal George.

Ushio Kitayama

Shizuku's father. Big shot in the business world. His business name is Ushio Kitagata.

Benio Kitayama

Shizuku's mother. An A-rank magician who was once renowned for her vibration magic.

Wataru Kitayama

Shizuku's younger brother. Sixth grade. Dearly loves his older sister. Aims to be a magic engineer.

Harumi Naruse

Shizuku's older cousin. Student at National Magic University Fourth Affiliated High School.

Gouki Ichijou

Masaki's father. Current head of the Ichijou, one of the Ten Master Clans.

Midori Ichijou

Masaki's mother. Warm and good at cooking.

Akane Ichijou

Eldest daughter of the Ichijou. Masaki's younger sister. Enrolled in an elite private middle school this year. Likes Shinkurou.

Ruri Ichijou

Second daughter of the Ichijou. Masaki's younger sister. Stable and does things her own way.

Ushiyama

Manager of Four Leaves. Technology's CAD R & D Section 3. A person in whom Tatsuya places his trust.

Ernst Rosen

A prominent CAD manufacturer. President of Rosen Magicraft's Japanese branch.

Toshikazu Chiba

Erika Chiba's oldest brother. Has a career in the Ministry of Police. A playboy at first glance.

Retsu Kudou

Renowned as the strongest magician in the world. Given the honorary title of Sage.

Naotsugu Chiba

Erika Chiba's second-oldest brother. Mari's lover. Possesses full mastery of the Chiba (thousand blades) style of kenjutsu. Nicknamed "Kirin Child of the Chiba."

Makoto Kudou

Son of Retsu Kudou, elder of Japan's magic world, and current head of the Kudou family.

Inagaki

An inspector with the Ministry of Police. Toshikazu Chiba's subordinate.

Minoru Kudou

Makoto's son. Freshman at National Magic University Second Affiliated High School, but hardly attends due to frequent illness. Also Kyouko Fujibayashi's younger brother by a different father.

Anna Rosen Katori

Erika's mother. Half Japanese and half German, was the mistress of Erika's father, the current leader of the Chiba.

Mamoru Kuki

One of the Eighteen Support Clans. Follows the Kudou family. Calls Retsu Kudou "Sensei" out of respect.

Maki Sawamura

A female actress who has been nominated for best leading female actress by distinguished movie awards. Acknowledged not only for her beauty but also her acting skills.

Kouichi Saegusa

Mayumi's father and the current leader of the Saegusa. Also a top-top-class magician.

Saburou Nakura

A powerful magician employed by the Saegusa family. Mainly serves as Mayumi's personal bodyguard.

Harunobu Kazama

Commanding officer of the 101st Brigade's Independent Magic Battalion. Ranked major.

Shigeru Sanada

Executive officer of the 101st Brigade's Independent Magic Battalion. Ranked captain.

Kyouko Fujibayashi

Female officer serving as Kazama's aide. Ranked second lieutenant.

Hiromi Saeki

Brigadier general of the Japan Ground Defense Force's 101st Brigade. Ranked major general. Superior officer to Harunobu Kazama, commanding officer of the Independent Magic Battalion. Due to her appearance, she is also known as the Silver Fox.

Muraji Yanagi

Executive officer of the 101st Brigade's Independent Magic Battalion. Ranked captain.

Kousuke Yamanaka

Executive officer of the 101st Brigade's Independent Magic Battalion. Physician ranked major. First-rate healing magician.

Sakai

Belongs to the Japan Ground Defense Force's general headquarters. Ranked colonel. Seen as staunchly anti–Great Asian Alliance.

Gongjin Zhou

A handsome young man who brought Lu and Chen to Yokohama. A mysterious figure who hangs out in Chinatown.

Xiangshan Chen

Leader of the Great Asian Alliance Army's Special Covert Forces. Has a heartless personality.

Ganghu Lu

The ace magician of the Great Asian Alliance Army's Special Covert Forces. Also known as the "Man-Eating Tiger."

Rin

A girl Morisaki saved. Her full name is Meiling Sun. The new leader of the Hong Kong–based international crime syndicate No-Head Dragon.

Miya Shiba

Tatsuya and Miyuki's actual mother. Deceased. The only magician skilled in mental construction interference magic.

Honami Sakurai

Miya's Guardian. Deceased. Part of the first generation of the Sakura series, engineered magicians with strengthened magical capacity through genetic modification.

Sayuri Shiba

Tatsuya and Miyuki's stepmother. Dislikes them.

Mitsugu Kuroba

Miya Shiba and Maya Yotsuba's cousin. Father of Ayako and Fumiya.

Ayako Kuroba

Tatsuya and Miyuki's second cousin. Has a younger twin brother named Fumiya. Student at Fourth High.

Fumiya Kuroba

A candidate for next head of the Yotsuba. Tatsuya and Miyuki's second cousin. Has an older twin sister named Ayako. Student at Fourth High.

Maya Yotsuba

Tatsuya and Miyuki's aunt. Miya's younger twin sister. The current head of the Yotsuba.

Hayama

An elderly butler employed to Maya.

Yuuka Tsukuba

A candidate to become the next leader of the Yotsuba clan. Twenty-two years old. Former vice president of the First High's student council. Currently a senior attending the Magic University. Strong in mental interference magic.

Katsushige Shibata

A candidate to become the next leader of the Yotsuba clan. Employed by the Ministry of Defense. An alum of Fifth High. Specializes in convergence magic.

Kotona Tsutsumi

One of Katsushige Shibata's Guardians. A second-generation Bard series engineered magician. Specializes in sound-based magic.

Kanata Tsutsumi

One of Katsushige Shibata's Guardians. A second-generation Bard series engineered magician. Like his older sister, Kotona, he specializes in sound-based magic.

Angelina Kudou Shields

Commander of the USNA's magician unit, the Stars. Rank is major. Nickname is Lina. Also one of the Thirteen Apostles, strategic magicians.

Virginia Balance

The USNA Joint Chiefs of Staff Information Bureau Internal Inspection Office's first deputy commissioner. Ranked colonel. Came to Japan in order to support Lina.

Silvia Mercury First

A planet-class magician in the USNA's magician unit, the Stars. Rank is warrant officer. Her nickname is Silvia, and Mercury First is her codename. During their mission in Japan, she serves as Major Sirius's aide.

Benjamin Canopus

Number two in the USNA's magician unit, the Stars. Rank is major. Takes command when Major Sirius is absent.

Mikaela Hongou

An agent sent into Japan by the USNA (although her real job is magic scientist for the Department of Defense). Nicknamed Mia.

Claire

Hunter Q—a female soldier in the magician unit Stardust for those who couldn't be Stars. Q refers to the 17th of the pursuit unit.

Alfred Fomalhaut

A first-degree star magician in the USNA's magician unit, the Stars. Rank is first lieutenant. Nicknamed Freddie. Currently AWOL.

Rachel

Hunter R—a female soldier in the magician unit Stardust for those who couldn't be Stars. R refers to the 18th of the pursuit unit.

Charles Sullivan

A satellite-class magician in the USNA's magician unit, the Stars. Called by the codename Deimos Second. Currently AWOL.

Raymond S. Clark

A student at the high school in Berkeley, USNA, that Shizuku studies abroad at. A Caucasian boy who wastes no time making advances on Shizuku. Is secretly one of the Seven Sages.

Gu Jie

One of the Seven Sages. Also known as Gide Hague. A survivor of a Dahanese military's mage unit.

Glossary

Course 1 student emblem

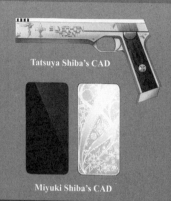

Tatsuya Shiba's CAD

Miyuki Shiba's CAD

Magic High School

Nickname for high schools affiliated with the National Magic University. There are nine schools throughout the nation. Of them, First High through Third High each adopt a system of Course 1 and Course 2 students to split up its two hundred incoming freshmen.

Blooms, Weeds

Slang terms used at First High to display the gap between Course 1 and Course 2 students. Course 1 student uniforms feature an eight-petaled emblem embroidered on the left breast, but Course 2 student uniforms do not.

CAD (Casting Assistant Device)

A device that simplifies magic casting. Magical programming is recorded within. There are many types and forms, some specialized and others multipurpose.

Four Leaves Technology (FLT)

A domestic CAD manufacturer. Originally more famous for magical-product engineering than for developing finished products, the development of the Silver model has made them much more widely known as a maker of CADs.

Taurus Silver

A genius engineer said to have advanced specialized CAD software by a decade in just a single year.

Eidos (individual information bodies)

Originally a term from Greek philosophy. In modern magic, *eidos* refers to the information bodies that accompany events. They form a so-called record of those events existing in the world, and can be considered the footprints of an object's state of being in the universe, be that active or passive. The definition of *magic* in its modern form is that of a technology that alters events by altering the information bodies composing them.

Idea (information body dimension)

Originally a term from Greek philosophy; pronounced "ee-dee-ah." In modern magic, *Idea* refers to the *platform* upon which information bodies are recorded—a spell, object, or energy's *dimension*. Magic is primarily a technology that outputs a magic program (a spell sequence) to affect the Idea (the dimension), which then rewrites the eidos (the individual bodies) recorded there.

Activation Sequence

The blueprints of magic, and the programming that constructs it. Activation sequences are stored in a compressed format in CADs. The magician sends a psionic wave into the CAD, which then expands the data and uses it to convert the activation sequence into a signal. This signal returns to the magician with the unpacked magic program.

Psions (thought particles)

Massless particles belonging to the dimension of spirit phenomena. These information particles record awareness and thought results. Eidos are considered the theoretical basis for modern magic, while activation sequences and magic programs are the technology forming its practical basis. All of these are bodies of information made up of psions.

Pushions (spirit particles)

Massless particles belonging to the dimension of spirit phenomena. Their existence has been confirmed, but their true form and function have yet to be elucidated. In general, magicians are only able to sense energized pushions. The technical term for them is *psycheons*.

Magician

An abbreviation of *magic technician*. *Magic technician* is the term for those with the skills to use magic at a practical level.

Magic program

An information body used to temporarily alter information attached to events. Constructed from psions possessed by the magician. Sometimes shortened to *magigram*.

Magic-calculation region

A mental region that constructs magic programs. The essential core of the talent of magic. Exists within the magician's unconscious regions, and though he or she can normally consciously use the magic-calculation region, they cannot perceive the processing happening within. The magic-calculation region may be called a black box, even for the magician performing the task.

Magic program output process

❶ Transmit an activation sequence to a CAD. This is called "reading in an activation sequence."

❷ Add variables to the activation sequence and send them to the magic-calculation region.

❸ Construct a magic program from the activation sequence and its variables.

❹ Send the constructed magic program along the "route"—between the lowest part of the conscious mind and highest part of the unconscious mind—then send it out the "gate" between conscious and unconscious, to output it onto the Idea.

❺ The magic program outputted onto the Idea interferes with the eidos at designated coordinates and overwrites them.

With a single-type, single-process spell, this five-stage process can be completed in under half a second. This is the bar for practical-level use with magicians.

Magic evaluation standards

The speed with which one constructs psionic information bodies is one's magical throughput, or processing speed. The scale and scope of the information bodies one can construct is one's magical capacity. The strength with which one can overwrite eidos with magic programs is one's influence. These three together are referred to as a person's magical power.

Cardinal Code hypothesis

A school of thought claiming that within the four families and eight types of magic, there exist foundational plus and minus magic programs, for sixteen in all, and that by combining these sixteen, one can construct every possible typed spell.

Typed magic

Any magic belonging to the four families and eight types.

Exotyped magic

A term for spells that control mental phenomena rather than physical ones. Encompasses many fields, from divine magic and spirit magic—which employs spiritual presences—to mind reading, astral form separation, and consciousness control.

Ten Master Clans

The most powerful magician organization in Japan. The ten families are chosen every four years from among twenty-eight: Ichijou, Ichinokura, Isshiki, Futatsugi, Nikaidou, Nihei, Mitsuya, Mikazuki, Yotsuba, Itsuwa, Gotou, Itsumi, Mutsuzuka, Rokkaku, Rokugou, Roppongi, Saegusa, Shippou, Tanabata, Nanase, Yatsushiro, Hassaku, Hachiman, Kudou, Kuki, Kuzumi, Juumonji, and Tooyama.

Numbers

Just like the Ten Master Clans contain a number from one to ten in their surname, well-known families in the Hundred Families use numbers eleven or greater, such as Chiyoda (thousand), Isori (fifty), and Chiba (thousand). The value isn't an indicator of strength, but the fact that it is present in the surname is one measure to broadly judge the capacity of a magic family by their bloodline.

Non-numbers

Also called Extra Numbers, or simply Extras. Magician families who have been stripped of their number. Once, when magicians were weapons and experimental samples, this was a stigma between the success cases, who were given numbers, and the failure cases, who didn't display good enough results.

Various Spells

• Cocytus

Outer magic that freezes the mind. A frozen mind cannot order the flesh to die, so anyone subject to this magic enters a state of mental stasis, causing their body to stop. Partial crystallization of the flesh is sometimes observed because of the interaction between mind and body.

• Rumbling

An old spell that vibrates the ground as a medium for a spirit, an independent information body.

• Program Dispersion

A spell that dismantles a magic program, the main component of a spell, into a group of psionic particles with no meaningful structure. Since magic programs affect the information bodies associated with events, it is necessary for the information structure to be exposed, leaving no way to prevent interference against the magic program itself.

• Program Demolition

A typeless spell that rams a mass of compressed psionic particles directly into an object without going through the Idea, causing it to explode and blow away the psion information bodies recorded in magic, such as activation sequences and magic programs. It may be called magic, but because it is a psionic bullet without any structure as a magic program for altering events, it isn't affected by Information Boost or Area Interference. The pressure of the bullet itself will also repel any Cast Jamming effects. Because it has zero physical effect, no obstacle can block it.

• Mine Origin

A magic that imparts strong vibrations to anything with a connotation of "ground"—such as dirt, crag, sand, or concrete—regardless of material.

• Fissure

A spell that uses spirits, independent information bodies, as a medium to push a line into the ground, creating the appearance of a fissure opening in the earth.

• Dry Blizzard

A spell that gathers carbon dioxide from the air, creates dry-ice particles, then converts the extra heat energy from the freezing process to kinetic energy to launch the dry-ice particles at a high speed.

• Slithering Thunders

In addition to condensing the water vapor from Dry Blizzard's dry-ice evaporation and creating a highly conductive mist with the evaporated carbon dioxide in it, this spell creates static electricity with vibration-type magic and emission-type magic. A combination spell, it also fires an electric attack at an enemy using the carbon gas-filled mist and water droplets as a conductor.

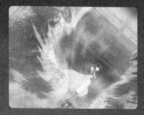

• Niflheim

A vibration- and deceleration-type area-of-effect spell. It chills a large volume of air, then moves it to freeze a wide range. In blunt terms, it creates a super-large refrigerator. The white mist that appears upon activation is the particles of frozen ice and dry ice, but at higher levels, a mist of frozen liquid nitrogen occurs.

• Burst

A dispersion-type spell that vaporizes the liquid inside a target object. When used on a creature, the spell will vaporize bodily fluids and cause the body to rupture. When used on a machine powered by internal combustion, the spell vaporizes the fuel and makes it explode. Fuel cells see the same result, and even if no burnable fuel is on board, there is no machine that does not contain some liquid, such as battery fluid, hydraulic fluid, coolant, or lubricant; once Burst activates, virtually any machine will be destroyed.

• Disheveled Hair

An old spell that, instead of specifying a direction and changing the wind's direction to that, uses air current control to bring about the vague result of "tangling" it, causing currents along the ground that entangle an opponent's feet in the grass. Only usable on plains with grass of a certain height.

Magic Swords

Aside from fighting techniques that use magic itself as a weapon, another method of magical combat involves techniques for using magic to strengthen and control weapons. The majority of these spells combine magic with projectile weapons such as guns and bows, but the art of the sword, known as *kenjutsu*, has developed in Japan as well as a way to link magic with sword techniques. This has led to magic technicians formulating personal-use magic techniques known as magic swords, which can be said to be both modern magic and old magic.

1. High-Frequency Blade

A spell that locally liquefies a solid body and cleaves it by causing a blade to vibrate at a high speed, then propagate the vibration that exceeds the molecular cohesive force of matter it comes in contact with. Used as a set with a spell to prevent the blade from breaking.

2. Pressure Cut

A spell that generates left-right perpendicular repulsive force relative to the angle of a slashing blade edge, causing the blade to force apart any object it touches and thereby cleave it. The size of the repulsive field is less than a millimeter, but it has the strength to interfere with light, so when seen from the front, the blade edge becomes a black line.

3. Douji-Giri (Simultaneous Cut)

An old-magic spell passed down as a secret sword art of the Genji. It is a magic sword technique wherein the user remotely manipulates two blades through a third in their hands in order to have the swords surround an opponent and slash simultaneously. *Douji* is the Japanese pronunciation for both "simultaneous" and "child," so this ambiguity was used to keep the inherited nature of the technique a secret.

4. Zantetsu (Iron Cleaver)

A secret sword art of the Chiba clan. Rather than defining a katana as a hulk of steel and iron, this movement spell defines it as a single concept, then the spell moves the katana along a slashing path set by the magic program. The result is that the katana is defined as a mono-molecular blade, never breaking, bending, or chipping as it slices through any objects in its path.

5. Jinrai Zantetsu (Lightning Iron Cleaver)

An expanded version of Zantetsu that makes use of the Ikazuchi-Maru, a personal-armament device. By defining the katana and its wielder as one collective concept, the spell executes the entire series of actions, from enemy contact to slash, incredibly quickly and with faultless precision.

6. Mountain Tsunami

A secret sword art of the Chiba clan that makes use of the Orochi-Maru, a giant personal weapon six feet long. The user minimizes their own inertia and that of their katana while approaching an enemy at a high speed and, at the moment of impact, adds the neutralized inertia to the blade's inertia and slams the target with it. The longer the approach run, the greater the false inertial mass, reaching a maximum of ten tons.

7. *Usuba Kagerou* (Antlion)

A spell that uses hardening magic to anchor a five-nanometer-thick sheet of woven carbon nanotube to a perfect surface and make it a blade. The blade that *Usuba Kagerou* creates is sharper than any sword or razor, but the spell contains no functions to support moving the blade, demanding technical sword skill and ability from the user.

Magic Technician Development Institutes

Laboratories for the purpose of magician development that the Japanese government established one after another in response to the geopolitical climate, which had become strained prior to World War III in the 2030s. Their objectives were not to develop magic but specifically to develop magicians, researching various methods to give birth to human specimens who were most suitable for areas of magic that were considered important, including, but not limited to, genetic engineering.

Ten magic technician development institutes were established, numbered as such, and even today, five are still in operation.

The details of each institute's research are described below.

Magic Technician Development Institute One

Established in Kanazawa in 2031. Currently shut down.

Its research focus, revolving around close combat, was the development of magic that directly manipulated biological organisms. The vaporization spell Burst is derived from this facility's research. Notably, magic that could control a human body's movements was forbidden as it enabled puppet terrorism (suicide attacks using victims that had been turned into puppets).

Magic Technician Development Institute Two

Established on Awaji Island in 2031. Currently in operation.

Develops opposite magic to that of Lab One: magic that can manipulate inorganic objects, especially absorption-type spells related to oxidation-reduction reactions.

Magic Technician Development Institute Three

Established in Atsugi in 2032. Currently in operation.

With its goal of developing magicians who can react to a variety of situations when operating independently, this facility is the main driver behind the research on multicasting. In particular, it tests the limits of how many spells are possible during simultaneous casting and continual casting and develops magicians who can simultaneously cast multiple spells.

Magic Technician Development Institute Four

Details unknown. Its location is speculated to be near the old prefectural border between Tokyo and Yamanashi. Its establishment is believed to have occurred in 2033. It is assumed to be shut down, but the truth of that matter is unknown. Lab Four is rumored to be the only magic research facility that was established not only with government support but also investment from private sponsors who held strong influence over the nation; it is currently operating without government oversight and being managed directly by those sponsors. Rumors also say that those sponsors actually took over control of the facility before the 2020s.

It is said their goal is to use mental interference magic to strengthen the very wellspring of the talent called magic, which exists in a magician's unconscious—the magic calculation region itself.

Magic Technician Development Institute Five

Established in Uwajima, Shikoku, in 2035. Currently in operation.

Researches magic that can manipulate various forms of matter. Its main focus, fluid control, is not technically difficult, but it has also succeeded in manipulating various solid forms. The fruits of its research include Bahamut, a spell jointly developed with the USNA. Along with the fluid-manipulation spell Abyss, it is known internationally as a magic research facility that developed two strategic-class spells.

Magic Technician Development Institute Six

Established in Sendai in 2035. Currently in operation.

Researches magical heat control. Along with Lab Eight, it gives the impression of being a facility more for basic research than military purposes. However, it is said that they conducted the most genetic manipulation experiments out of all the magic technician development institutes, aside from Lab Four. (Though, of course, the full accounting of Lab Four's situation is not possible.)

Magic Technician Development Institute Seven

Established in Tokyo in 2036. Currently shut down.

Developed magic with an emphasis on anti-group combat. It successfully created colony control magic. Contrary to Lab Six, which was largely a nonmilitary organization, Lab Seven was established as a magician development research facility that could be relied on for assistance in defending the capital in case of an emergency.

Magic Technician Development Institute Eight

Established in Kitakyushu in 2037. Currently in operation.

Researches magical control of gravitational force, electromagnetic force, strong force, and weak force. It is a pure research institute to a greater extent than even Lab Six. However, unlike Lab Six, its relationship to the JDF is steadfast. This is because Lab Eight's research focus can be easily linked to nuclear weapons development, (though they currently avoid such connotations thanks to the JDF's seal of approval).

Magic Technician Development Institute Nine

Established in Nara in 2037. Currently shut down.

This facility tried to solve several problems modern magic struggled with, such as fuzzy spell manipulation, through a fusion of modern and ancient magic, integrating ancient know-how into modern magic.

Magic Technician Development Institute Ten

Established in Tokyo in 2039. Currently shut down.

Like Lab Seven, doubled as capital defense, researching area magic that could create virtual structures in space as a means of defending against high-firepower attacks. It resulted in a myriad of anti-physical barrier spells.

Lab Ten also aimed to raise magic abilities through different means from Lab Four. In precise terms, rather than enhancing the magic calculation region itself, they grappled with developing magicians who responded as needed by temporarily overclocking their magic calculation regions to use powerful magic. Whether their research was successful has not been made public.

Aside from these ten institutes, other laboratories with the goal of developing Elements were operational from the 2010s to the 2020s, but they are currently all shut down. In addition, the JDF possesses a secret research facility directly under the Ground Defense Force's General Headquarters' jurisdiction, established in 2002, which is still carrying on its research. Retsu Kudou underwent enhancement operations at this institution before moving to Lab Nine.

Strategic Magicians: The Thirteen Apostles

Because modern magic was born into a highly technological world, only a few nations were able to develop strong magic for military purposes. As a result, only a handful were able to develop "strategic magic," which rivaled weapons of mass destruction.

However, these nations shared the magic they developed with their allies, and certain magicians of allied nations with high aptitudes for strategic magic came to be known as strategic magicians.

As of April 2095, there are thirteen magicians publicly recognized as strategic magicians by their nations. They are called the Thirteen Apostles and are seen as important factors in the world's military balance. The Thirteen Apostles' nations, names, and strategic spell names are listed below.

USNA

Angie Sirius: Heavy Metal Burst
Elliott Miller: Leviathan
Laurent Barthes: Leviathan
* The only one belonging to the Stars is Angie Sirius. Elliott Miller is stationed at Alaska Base, and Laurent Barthes outside the country at Gibraltar Base, and for the most part, they don't move.

New Soviet Union

Igor Andreivich Bezobrazov: Tuman Bomba
Leonid Kondratenko: Zemlja Armija
* As Kondratenko is of advanced age, he generally stays at the Black Sea Base.

Great Asian Alliance

Yunde Liu: Pilita (Thunderclap Tower)
* Yunde Liu died in the October 31, 2095, battle against Japan.

Indo-Persian Federation

Barat Chandra Khan: Agni Downburst

Japan

Mio Itsuwa: Abyss

Brazil

Miguel Diez: Synchroliner Fusion
* This magic program was named by the USNA.

England

William MacLeod: Ozone Circle

Germany

Karla Schmidt: Ozone Circle
* Ozone Circle is based on a spell codeveloped by nations in the EU before its split as a means to fix the hole in the ozone layer. The magic program was perfected by England and then publicized to the old EU through a convention.

Turkey

Ali Sahin: Bahamut
* This magic program was developed in cooperation with the USNA and Japan, then provided to Turkey by Japan.

Thailand

Somchai Bunnag: Agni Downburst
* This magic program was provided by Indo-Persia.

The International Situation
State of the World in 2096

West EU and East EU are allied states, but nations are independent

New Soviet Union

Japan, Mongolia, and Kazakhstan are in an alliance

Japan

USNA (United States of North America)

Indo-Persian Federation

Great Asian Alliance

Arab Alliance

Taiwan is an independent nation

African Continent (southwestern portions are mostly lawless)

Southeast Asian Alliance (includes Taiwan, the Philippines, and New Guinea)

Brazil

Other nations have broken into regional local governments

World War III, also called the Twenty Years' Global War Outbreak, was directly triggered by global cooling, and it fundamentally redrew the world map.

The USA annexed Canada and the countries from Mexico to Panama to form the United States of North America, or the USNA.

Russia reabsorbed Ukraine and Belarus to form the New Soviet Union.

China conquered northern Burma, northern Vietnam, northern Laos, and the Korean Peninsula to form the Great Asian Alliance, or GAA.

India and Iran absorbed several central Asian countries (Turkmenistan, Uzbekistan, Tajikistan, and Afghanistan) and South Asian countries (Pakistan, Nepal, Bhutan, Bangladesh, and Sri Lanka) to form the Indo-Persian Federation.

The other Asian and Arab countries formed regional military alliances to resist the three superpowers: the New Soviet Union, GAA, and the Indo-Persian Federation.

Australia chose national isolation.

The EU failed to unify and split into an eastern and a western section bordered by Germany and France. These east-west groupings also failed to form unions and now are actually weaker than they were before unification.

Africa saw half its nations destroyed altogether, with the surviving ones barely managing to retain urban control.

South America, excluding Brazil, fell into small, isolated states administered on a local government level.

The Irregular at
Magic High School

[1]

The chimes rang, ending the day's classes.

Despite school now being conducted online, which removed the teachers and their watchful gazes from classrooms, the feeling of release that came with the end of the school day went unchanged.

And today, campus was especially abuzz.

It was no surprise: Today was Tuesday, December 25, 2096—the last day of the second term of the 2096 academic year.

The only thing that set it apart from a normal day was that classes ended midmorning. There were no formalities that could be considered a commencement ceremony. There was also no public presentation of academic results. Grades were a wholly personal matter and guardians were only contacted if they threatened a student's academic progression or graduation.

Nevertheless, once the students had access to their grades, which included pass-fail general education subjects, two distinct categories of students appeared in the halls of First High: those in high spirits and those with slumping shoulders.

Although the newly established magic engineering class of 2-E was special in some regards, it was no exception when it came to grades. While being in the engineering course meant that the cohort was excepted from a certain degree of worry over their practical-skill grades, Tatsuya and many of his classmates were still concerned about accruing sufficient credits to graduate.

Once Tatsuya Shiba had confirmed that his grades were satisfactory, he downloaded them to his portable terminal and stood—whereupon he felt a piercing gaze coming from beside him.

"Yes, Mizuki?"

"Um, er…nothing!" she hedged nervously.

Mizuki had wanted to ask Tatsuya the entirely reasonable question of how his grades had turned out but then realized that doing so would raise the question of what her own had been, and she had thought better of it at the last moment. Mizuki herself was among the top half of the students in the class, but she still didn't have the courage to disclose her own grades right after hearing Tatsuya's.

"Oh? All right. Well, see you later."

"Yes! Later, then!"

After exchanging pleasantries, Tatsuya made for the student council room while Mizuki headed to the art room.

By 5:00 PM, it was quite dark. After finishing their student council and club activities, Tatsuya and his friends gathered at Einebrise. The café was just off the main road that led to the school, and it had become firmly established as their hangout spot. That said, this typically amounted to only a short while spent there before continuing home from school, and as the group wasn't rowdy and didn't leave messes behind, the staff had come to regard them as regulars.

"Now then," prompted Erika, "it's a day late, but nevertheless, all together now: *Merry Christmas!*"

""Merry Christmas!"" the group chorused.

Tatsuya and his friends had reserved Einebrise as the venue for their belated Christmas party.

"Glad everyone's in good spirits! Although if I'm honest, I wanted to say it while the sun was still up."

"Well, we didn't have much choice. Everybody had club activities—even you, Erika," Miyuki reassured.

Erika grinned sheepishly. "I don't get in trouble if I bow out of club stuff before it really wraps up, but I guess that wouldn't fly for you, Miss Student Council President."

"It isn't just me," Miyuki went on. "Yoshida's the chief of the disciplinary committee, and Shizuku's doing her rotation on it, too."

Mikihiko laughed abashedly at being mentioned, and Shizuku gave a quick nod: "Mm-hmm."

"Yeah, that's true. Though Leo's got no excuse," Erika noted.

"Whaddaya mean by that?!" the boy squawked.

Ignoring him, Erika looked from Honoka to Tatsuya. "Honoka's on the student council, too, and Tatsuya's the secretary."

"It's all right, though. We all managed to get together, even if it was a day later than we wanted," Tatsuya replied, subtly trying to sidestep any contention.

"I guess." Erika nodded, blithely unaware of this. "There *were* a lot of people who had plans yesterday."

Shizuku had had to make an appearance at an event held by the company her father ran, and Honoka had been dragged along.

Mikihiko had been pulled into the party thrown by the younger generation of his clan. The female attendees outnumbered the male, and though Mikihiko had strongly resisted going, his older brother had stubbornly insisted that he needed "directorial assistance."

And indeed, Erika herself was among those whose family circumstances had interfered. In her case, though, she had been sent along with her oldest brother, Toshikazu, not to the Chiba family Christmas party but rather a party for the Kanto regional police. The two of them were showing up in place of their father, who had to attend a party being thrown by a prominent politician. Erika was unhappy at being assigned this duty despite still being treated as something of an embarrassment, but she knew that there was no percentage in lodging a complaint about it with her father, so she stoically accompanied her brother. If Toshikazu had had a wife or fiancée, this role surely wouldn't have been given to her at all, and Erika expressed her resentment with a constant drizzle of nasty remarks directed at her eldest brother.

Owing to all those circumstances, the friends were holding their own Christmas party today, a day late.

Incidentally, the attendees were: Tatsuya, Miyuki, Erika, Leo, Mizuki, Mikihiko, Honoka—all juniors. Minami had been invited to a different party by a classmate in class 1-C. Their circumstances seemed to be similar in that they hadn't been able to throw a proper party on Christmas Eve and were making up for it the day after. It was being held at a certain famous restaurant, and the food being served was several notches fancier than what Tatsuya and his friends were enjoying. Kasumi from class 1-C was also attending the soirée, and she'd brought Izumi along with her.

Kasumi and Izumi had no choice but to spend the previous night glad-handing at a party they'd been invited to by an employee from a subsidiary company of the Saegusa family, so Kasumi was undoubtedly determined to properly enjoy herself tonight. There was some fear that she'd enjoy herself too much, but her classmates would probably overlook a bit of mischief. It was likely that this calculation was part of why Izumi hadn't insisted on being at the same party as Miyuki.

Thus, Tatsuya and his friends had ended up in a small get-together consisting of only classmates.

Unlike the party Minami was attending, there were no plans for a full dinner. Each attendee received a slice of cake, with the café's chef focusing more on taste and quality than volume. It was easier to hold a conversation when not preoccupied by eating and drinking. Of course, an objection to this was expected from somewhere in Leo's vicinity, but it was undeniable that conversation flowed smoothly for a solid hour and a half, right up until just before 7:00 PM.

"Another year's almost over," Mizuki murmured poignantly as

the end of the party's reserved time approached, her voice low so as not to disturb the cheerful chatter around her.

"Another peaceful year, huh?" cheerfully replied Erika, almost as if she was allergic to sentimentality.

"Was it, though? Honestly, it seemed pretty rough," Mikihiko said with obvious sincerity, which primed the pump.

"Yeah, there *was* the whole vampire uprising," Honoka noted innocently.

"And the incident with Pixie's confession," Shizuku quipped immediately after, which drew a round of laughter from the table.

"Shizuku! Stop it, geez!" Honoka protested—but poor Honoka notwithstanding, it was a pretty good joke.

"Not to take Erika's side or anything, but we had an easier time this year than the last. Nothing as bad as the Yokohama incident or anything hit us," Leo added.

"If that kind of thing is gonna happen every year, I'm out," Tatsuya shot back with a grin.

"Y'know, that's totally fair," Leo agreed, and everyone else laughed in agreement.

"Tatsuya?"

The party displayed impeccable manners—mostly meaning they vacated their table and left the café promptly at 7:00 PM. As they were exiting, Tatsuya heard Honoka's voice at his back.

"Would you like to visit a temple on New Year's Day with me again this year?" she finished.

He'd looked over his shoulder at the sound of his name, and before getting a chance to respond, he'd already received an invitation. "Ah, New Year's?"

"Oh, I—I mean!" Honoka immediately started waving her hands around in a panic. "With everyone, I mean! Not just the two of us! Shizuku's here now, and Erika said she'd come along."

Evidently, Honoka had already done a fair amount of organizing this outing. She was really enthusiastic about it. Tatsuya could tell she wasn't asking on impulse.

Which made Tatsuya feel even worse about his answer: "...Sorry, but I can't. Miyuki and I have a thing this New Year's Day that we absolutely can't miss."

Honoka looked deeply shocked. It hadn't occurred to her that he'd refuse.

"I really appreciate the invita—"

"It's fine," Honoka said with a strained smile before Tatsuya could finish. "It's something really important, isn't it? Don't worry about it."

Her composure was obviously forced, but she'd gotten those words out without her voice wavering.

Tatsuya couldn't ignore the obvious concern she'd shown for him thus far, though. "Invite me along another time, though, okay?" he said, rather than apologizing.

This was enough to dispel any ill feelings between Tatsuya and Honoka. But as Miyuki stood next to Tatsuya, her eyes remained downcast.

"What's wrong, Miyuki?" Shizuku asked, noticing immediately. The Shiba sister's already pale skin had lost all of its color, and she almost looked ill. Shizuku noticed as much. "Do you feel unwell?"

"...No, I'm fine. Thank you," Miyuki whispered.

Despite what she said, her face was still sickly and her smile weak. While the elegant and delicate look did match Miyuki's aesthetic, her friend couldn't just bring that up, especially in light of the sudden change.

On the other hand, Erika didn't seem particularly concerned by Miyuki's appearance. "Aw, c'mon, you don't have to be *that* sad about missing out on the trip to the temple. I didn't have much going on this year, but I still totally flaked. Plus, you've got something really important going on, right? Honoka said it herself. Just get in touch when it's over. We'll all go out somewhere."

Erika didn't care any less about her friends than Shizuku—she just knew that if Miyuki was suffering from a physical affliction serious enough to need treatment, Tatsuya would take care of it. And since he wasn't, Erika reckoned that Miyuki's problem had to be something psychological, and that's why she decided to try lightening the mood.

"That's true. Once we're free, we'll contact you," said Miyuki with a somewhat more genuine smile. Nevertheless, the pallor that had stolen her skin's vitality remained.

Miyuki's affliction was temporary, and by the time they returned home, her face had regained its color.

Erika's deduction had been correct: Miyuki's discomfort had not been caused by any physical condition. This was immediately clear to Tatsuya.

The real cause was psychological shock. Over the past few days, Miyuki had been so anxious over the impending plans for New Year's Day that the very mention of it had caused an automatic reaction—essentially, the fact that it had been called to mind unbidden was enough to inspire alarm. Tatsuya knew this as well.

Which was why he made her a suggestion despite the party's light appetizer and dessert being far from enough for dinner. "Miyuki, why not rest in your room for a little while? We can eat later."

"How could I, when you're—!" she shot back, but she soon caught herself, realizing that her current condition wasn't helping anyone. But instead of simply accepting his offer, she wanted to make sure he didn't mind waiting for dinner until later. "…No, you're right. Could I rest for an hour or so?"

"Of course. I'm the one who said you should, right?" answered Tatsuya with a smile. "And no—Miyuki, you should rest until you're feeling better," he added quickly.

"All right, Brother. I'll do as you say." Miyuki gave a small bow, her guilt considerably reduced now that she had been *ordered* to rest.

* * *

Her second-floor bedroom was chilly with midwinter's cold. Even well-insulated modern construction struggled to preserve interior warmth for more than twelve hours through the late December nights.

Of course, thanks to automation, the residence could be set to turn up the heat in advance before the homeowners returned. Such technology was, by now, ubiquitous.

But Miyuki had never used this function. She had no need to.

She opened the door to her room and glanced inside. That was all it took to raise the temperature to an acceptable level. She didn't even need a CAD's help for magic that simple. Still, once Miyuki entered her room and closed the door, she turned the heater on—at the end of the day, indefinitely maintaining the room's temperature at a constant level was a task better suited to HVAC than magic.

That taken care of, she shrugged off her coat and school uniform.

No matter how tired she was at the end of the day, she never left her clothes lying on her bed or a chair. Coats, blazers, nightgowns, and dresses alike were all neatly hung in her closet, ready to be sifted through whenever the next day's outfit needed to be found. As she was slipping her arm through the sleeve of a long-hemmed, loose-fitting one-piece dress she rarely wore inside the house, her gaze fell upon the letter rack on her desk.

Once she finished changing in front of the room's mirror, Miyuki sat down at her desk, then reached into her letter rack and pulled a single envelope from it.

She didn't have to check to know what was contained within. She had read every character and every word so many times she had them memorized, and yet she pulled the letter from the envelope as if compelled.

The contents came in the form of an invitation to a New Year's celebration held by the Yotsuba family—at which her participation was *demanded*.

Both the previous year and the year before it, Miyuki had visited the family headquarters for the New Year. However, she hadn't shown her face at the New Year's celebration where the heads of the various branch families gathered. The primary reason for this was that she simply hadn't been invited, but she had been happy to avoid both the celebration and the branch family heads. She couldn't stand the disrespect they showed her brother.

But this year, Maya had invited—no, *compelled*—her attendance. Indeed, Maya's own signature was on the invitation. No matter how disinclined Miyuki was to go, it was unavoidable. Regardless of how the branch house heads treated Tatsuya, she wouldn't be allowed to stop them. Miyuki was starting to worry just how much she would be able to endure.

But that was a minor detail compared with a greater anxiety, from which she saw no escape:

Miyuki felt a deepening certainty about why she had been summoned to appear before the family heads.

Her aunt finally intended to name her successor.

Her aunt intended to name *her* as successor.

Miyuki no longer had any desire to take the role.

Once, yes, she had hoped to be worthy to lead the clan. But after a certain summer's day four years ago, even that ambition had left her.

She had never particularly wanted the role itself—she had simply wanted the adults around her to continue telling her that she was worthy of it. And in a way, perhaps she still wanted that.

The head of the Yotsuba family would become the most prominent magician—although not necessarily the most powerful—of the generation. There were four candidates for the position still in the running: Miyuki Shiba, Fumiya Kuroba, Yuuka Tsukuba, and Katsushige Shibata. Of them, Miyuki was the best magician. The family's servants had always said so.

The head butler, Hayama, the second butler, a fixer named Hanabishi, and the third butler, Kurebayashi, who was in charge of coordination and facilities for magicians and functioned almost like the Yotsuba clan's nerve center—these were people who didn't drop such pronouncements lightly. But the servants under them often complimented Miyuki on her ability quite innocently, not even trying to ingratiate themselves to her.

Miyuki herself was aware that of the four remaining candidates, her magical ability was the strongest. She was confident that this was not vanity or folly but an objective evaluation. But her desire to be considered worthy of it was simply proof that the Yotsuba family's logic had rubbed off on her. She had been convinced that because she was the strongest magician of her generation, it was only natural that she would be named successor.

But if anyone asked whether she actually wanted to *be* the successor, Miyuki would say she had no interest. Given the option to turn down the role, there was little doubt that's what she would choose, as the work of leading the family would keep her too busy to spend any time with her brother.

At the same time, Miyuki entertained no thoughts of refusing. The position held no attraction for her personally, but if holding it meant she could secure better treatment for Tatsuya, perhaps it wouldn't be such a bad thing.

Becoming the Guardian of the family head would at least force the servants to stop disparaging him. She'd be able to demand a certain amount of respect on his behalf from the branch families. More for her brother rather than herself, Miyuki felt that she could bear the burden of leading the Yotsuba.

It wasn't even the prospect of being named successor itself that depressed her. The problem was the marriage she would be expected to accept as a part of that role.

It was bad enough that magicians were encouraged to marry young. Unlike people to whom special circumstances applied, like her aunt Maya or Mio Itsuwa, she would not be permitted to remain single. Magicians publicly acknowledged the importance of fundamental human rights, so there wouldn't be any legal consequences for remaining unmarried. But if she insisted on it, she was certain to be shunned by her community of magicians. The Yotsuba family was regarded by outsiders as lofty and high-handed, but as a member of one of the ten families who led Japan's magical society, she didn't have the luxury of ignoring her social reputation.

Given those circumstances and the fact that Maya had not married, the nation's ten leading families would seek a quick match for the next Yotsuba family head. Even if she weren't forced into marriage immediately upon being named the successor, an engagement would certainly be foisted upon her.

She would have to marry someone—who was not Tatsuya.

She would have to be the wife of someone—who was not Tatsuya.

On that count, Miyuki had no illusions. Given that a marriage to her biological brother would never be allowed, and given that as a magician, she would not be permitted to remain single, Miyuki had resigned herself to the reality that she would marry a man who was not him.

Miyuki refolded the letter and slipped it back inside its envelope, then replaced it in the letter rack and stood.

She sat in front of her vanity and silently addressed her reflection... *That's right. This is unavoidable. There's nothing I can do about it.*

The Miyuki in the mirror silently responded, *Is it really unavoidable? Or are you just resigned to it?* Somehow, her mirror-self's voice sounded younger.

That's right. The simple fact is that Tatsuya and I are siblings. There's nothing I can do but accept it, so I have. I'm resigned, replied Miyuki to her mirror-self.

Liar! I haven't accepted a thing! Just as Mirror-Miyuki was a bit younger, she was a bit more honest about her real feelings.

No matter how much we don't want to accept this, we must. Brother and I are genuine, biological siblings.

We're going to give up just because he's our brother?!

It's not a question of whether we give up or not. Siblings cannot marry. We've always known that, and we've never hoped that our brother would love us as a woman. You can't give up on something you never hoped for in the first place.

That's not true! If it is, how come we hate the idea of our fiancé, even though we've never seen him and don't even know if he exists?

Because if we marry and have children, we'll have to fulfill our duties as a mother before anything else. We won't be able to support and serve our brother. That's why we hate the idea.

We can just leave child-rearing to the servants. The head of the Yotsuba family doesn't have to attend to such menial labor themselves. And it's not like you'd be able to constantly be with your children anyway.

Miyuki stared evenly into the eyes of her mirror-self. She hadn't realized her own excuses would be so easy to dismantle.

The girl in the mirror continued, critical of Miyuki's refusal to face her own feelings in favor of maintaining appearances. *If you marry another man, there are still all sorts of ways you could be useful to Brother. You don't have to love a husband you took only to satisfy your obligations to magical society. So long as you fulfill your duty to have children, who could complain? No, Miyuki, what we hate is not the idea of marriage itself.*

Stop. Miyuki wanted to plug her ears.

Here's what we really think. What you really think.

Stop! She wanted to turn her back on the girl.

What you really hate…

But no matter how vehemently she shook her head, she couldn't stand and walk away from the mirror. *Stop…!*

…is the idea of being married to anyone other than Tatsuya.

She no longer had the heart to speak out against herself.

The idea of being taken by anyone other than Brother.

In the mirror, she saw her own terrified eyes. She saw her frightened self, a girl who'd tried so long not to think about this.

Never being his bride. Never making love to him. Never being able to love him as a woman! That's what you can't stand!

"Aah...!" A cry of distress slipped from her lips, and she collapsed from the chair in front of her vanity onto the floor. The mirror slipped from her field of vision, and the spell was broken.

"So what am I supposed to do?" As her thoughts came tumbling out, her divided feelings came back together. "We are brother and sister. We're biological siblings." One after another, the emotions she'd kept hidden within herself for so long flowed freely from her lips. "I'll never be allowed to love my brother that way. The world won't allow it. I'm sure he would think it a perversion, too. He'd be disgusted by me."

All alone in her room, the girl revealed the whole of her heart. There was no one to listen—which was why she was able to say anything at all.

What she said was not a confession to a priest.

What she said was not something that could be confided in another.

"I don't care what the world thinks of me. I don't care if they point at me behind my back or cast me out of society. But if my brother ever considers me repulsive...that would be unbearable!"

She didn't believe there was anything sinful about her feelings.

But there was only one person who could grant her forgiveness, and it was not God.

"...So there's nothing I can do about it."

Miyuki ended her confession with a decision. The words that emerged from deep inside her instead became tears that welled up and spilled from her eyes.

[2]

On the morning of the first day of the winter break, Tatsuya went to visit Four Leaves Technology's R & D Section 3, leaving Miyuki to mind the house with Minami.

R & D Section 3 was essentially his home turf, and for that reason, he knew that if he'd brought his sister along, she would have been quite welcome and not at all treated as an imposition. But he had the suspicion that on this particular day, he himself wouldn't have had any attention to spare, so he decided that it would be better to leave her be, relaxing at home.

And that was all because, today, Tatsuya planned to begin work on a new project. It wasn't development of a new CAD but rather the design of a large-scale system that would make full use of magic engineering technology. It would take years for the system to be implemented; what Tatsuya was trying to create would require energy, resources, and circumstances that FLT alone would never be able to arrange.

The project was called "ESCAPES," an acronym of "Extraction of both useful and harmful Substances from the Coastal Area of the Pacific using Electricity generated by a Stellar reactor." But the title was also meant in the literal sense: It was an escape method.

In the project's current state, all he could work on was completing the project protocols and the design of the systems that would go into it. Still, they had reached the point where the first step could finally be taken.

Tatsuya had had the vision for this project some three years earlier, in August of 2093, just a year after that fateful day in Okinawa. Loop casting, airborne devices, and the stellar generator were each components developed for this system, and a few days earlier, the final piece in the puzzle had come onto the horizon. There was still a lot of time left, both from the standpoint of the project's realization and Tatsuya's young age. Nevertheless, when he thought about what its realization would actually mean to him, he couldn't help but feel motivated in a way he never had before.

But only an hour into his work, he found his zeal doused. Just as he was finishing a project outline, surrounded by data so sensitive he wasn't allowed to transmit it even using quantum encryption, nor copy it to a data cube and bring it home to work on, he received an intercom call from a woman on R & D Section 3's staff.

"My apologies for interrupting, Prince."

He didn't particularly want to stop his work, but for staff to interrupt him when he was shut away in his workshop like this, it had to be something important. Tatsuya lifted his fingers from the keyboard and answered the incoming call. "What is it?"

"Sir, an individual named Mitsugu Kuroba is asking to see you."

Tatsuya frowned in spite of himself. So far as he was aware, Mitsugu had never visited FLT. His role in the Yotsuba organization was espionage, and as FLT was (one of) the Yotsubas' pure sources of funding, it was outside of his jurisdiction. Even if he did have some business with Tatsuya, there wasn't an obvious reason why he would need to pay this place a visit personally.

Tatsuya immediately determined that he didn't have enough information available to form a conjecture as to Mitsugu's motive. Whatever it was, he needed to meet Mitsugu and figure it out. Having decided as much, Tatsuya requested a meeting room that was unconnected to the online monitoring system. "I'll see him. Please arrange an offline meeting."

Upon entering the meeting room, Tatsuya locked the door before greeting his guest.

When Tatsuya turned back around, Mitsugu did not stand from the sofa where he sat. All he did to acknowledge Tatsuya's arrival was to remove the fedora he'd been fiddling with uneasily and place it on the sofa beside him.

"It's been a while, Mr. Kuroba. I haven't seen you since this past summer, I believe."

"Yeah." Mitsugu gave a sullen nod—and not just because the phrase *this past summer* called to mind the bitter memories of the grievous damage Gongjin Zhou had inflicted. Mitsugu's expression had been sour even before Tatsuya had arrived.

"May I sit?"

Mitsugu assented wordlessly, and Tatsuya sat down across from him, looking squarely at the other man's face. The difference in their age could have made them father and son, but Tatsuya's face betrayed not even a hint of deference, nor did he try to puff himself up.

Mitsugu's lip twisted in irritation. He looked on the verge of clicking his tongue in contempt.

Nonetheless, Mitsugu had no inclination to dismiss Tatsuya as "a mere glorified bodyguard." Although Tatsuya was the nephew of Maya Yotsuba, the current head of the Yotsuba family and the older brother of Miyuki, one of the candidates to become the next head, some among the Yotsuba clan—particularly the servants far removed from actual combat—found him easy to disparage, saying things like, "What good is someone with the Yotsuba blood running through their veins who can't even do proper magic?" and "They only gave him the job of guarding his sister out of pity."

But Mitsugu knew perfectly well that Tatsuya was more than that. It was true that in a conventional sense Tatsuya was deficient as a magician, but he had unusual abilities that more than made up for any of his defects.

Mitsugu found Tatsuya's bearing irritating for a single reason: It galled him to be treated as an equal by a boy the same age as his own son.

Mitsugu's expression gave no quarter. Indeed, if one of them could be said to be putting on any sort of airs, it was him.

"May I ask what business brings you here?" Tatsuya finally asked, after Mitsugu remained silent. "I'm rather busy, you see."

While the manner of asking wasn't particularly rude, the question itself, posed to an elder, was unmistakably so. But Mitsugu restrained himself. He was the one who'd come here uninvited, and he had enough perspective to know that losing his temper over something so minor would be disgraceful.

Mitsugu's statement contained only his demand, as though he were refusing to keep up any sort of appearance of propriety: "Recuse yourself from the New Year's celebration."

"I had no intention of attending in the first place."

"What...?" This answer was, apparently, completely outside of the man's expectations. The stony-faced expression he'd worn ever since Tatsuya entered the meeting room fell for the first time, replaced by one of honest surprise.

"I never expected or planned to attend the New Year's celebration. Miyuki is the one the family head ordered to attend."

Tatsuya referred to his aunt Maya as *the family head*. In doing so, he implied that Miyuki's attendance meant that she would be chosen as the next family head and, furthermore, that Mitsugu's interference was misplaced.

"Such quibbling...!" Mitsugu clicked his tongue, fully abandoning his previous effort to maintain decorum, such as it was. But his tone was a bit calmer now, either because Tatsuya wasn't the object of his ire or because he was simply running out of gas. "In that case, I ask that you persuade your sister not to attend."

The request's politeness did nothing to change whether Tatsuya was able to accommodate it, though. "Why don't you ask her yourself?"

Mitsugu had expected to be refused, but the direction of Tatsuya's answer was slightly different from what he'd anticipated. "If I were to ask her, I doubt your sister would agree to it. That's why I'm asking you to convince her."

"I'm not talking about Miyuki. Why don't you ask the family head to rescind the invitation?"

Mitsugu was momentarily stuck for an answer. "...I should think that goes without saying. I have protested that it is too soon many times to Maya."

"If that's true, then what point is there in asking me to stop Miyuki from attending the celebration? Even if she were to decline the invitation, the family head would hardly accept that."

Mitsugu fell silent at the irrefutable logic of Tatsuya's point.

A sly smile crept onto Tatsuya's face. "I don't blame you for thinking it's too soon, though. I'm sure you want Fumiya to get a bit more accomplished before you put him up as a candidate for head."

"Nonsense!" Mitsugu protested. His right hand came up from where it rested on his thigh and froze in a trembling clench from the effort required to resist his initial temptation to slam it down on the table in anger. "I've never had any inclination for Fumiya to assume leadership of the Yotsuba clan. His disposition is far too gentle, for one thing. In my view, as far as magical prowess goes, Miyuki is well suited to become the next head."

Tatsuya couldn't help but feel some surprise at this response. Until just now, he'd fully assumed that Mitsugu wanted Fumiya to become the next head.

But he set his own misunderstanding aside and instead attempted to discern Mitsugu's true aim. "All right, so in what way is it 'too soon,' then?"

Mitsugu hesitated to answer for a breath, instead regarding Tatsuya haughtily. "At the upcoming New Year's celebration, the next family head will be announced. And Maya intends to name Miyuki as her successor."

"I see," replied Tatsuya neutrally, as though hearing this information for the first time, even though it was what he'd expected.

"However, I believe that Miyuki's appointment as successor should be delayed until a certain important condition is dealt with. And I'm not the only one. Four families—the Shiiba, Mashiba, Shibata, and Shizuka—are of like mind on the matter."

"Meaning the branch families are in agreement, save for the Mugura and Tsukuba? So what is this condition?"

Mitsugu grinned unpleasantly. "Dealing with you." His eyes glittered with a darkness like tar. "In two more years, the Sakura-series-engineered magician Minami Sakurai will have gained enough power to be the Guardian of the Yotsuba clan. Even among the engineered employed by the clan, she is notable for her excellence. This would render you obsolete."

Mitsugu seemed uncharacteristically drunk on his own words as he continued. "Don't worry. We'll let you graduate from the Magic University. After that, you'll continue to contribute to the Yotsuba clan finances through your work as 'Taurus Silver.' There'll be no need for you to work for national defense, so you'll be released from your position as a special officer."

Mitsugu's eyes were still dark as the corners of his lips curled up. "Ah, right. Your father's shares in FLT will also be transferred to you. We can't very well reveal your existence to the public, so you can't be CEO, but you'll be the majority shareholder."

"Not like I have any interest in that," Tatsuya said tersely, cutting Mitsugu off. "None of what you've just described is within your power to decide on your own, Mr. Kuroba." *It will be Maya who decides*—he left the fact implied. "Making verbal promises like that, someone might start to suspect you of plotting rebellion."

"...I have no such intention." The dark smile on Mitsugu's face vanished, as though the spirit possessing him had released him. He looked down and fell silent, as though realizing he'd been acting abnormally.

"Mr. Kuroba, it will be my aunt, the head of the family, who decides whether Miyuki will attend the New Year's celebration. Neither Miyuki nor I can promise her absence on our own. Is that, at least, clear enough?"

"Nonetheless," the man said, his downcast eyes fixed on the table between them, "I don't want to make Fumiya or Ayako unhappy."

Tatsuya's eyes narrowed piercingly. "Is that so?"

Mitsugu looked up and met Tatsuya's gaze accusingly. "I said as much, did I not? I won't do anything."

"So you're simply waiting for your opportunity, then."

"I'm neutral. I'm no friend of yours, but for my children's sake, I won't move against you," he said past gritted teeth.

Tatsuya processed this information as a given. "I suppose if I were to ask you why you'd go to such lengths to distance me from my sister, you wouldn't tell me."

Mitsugu stood. Instead of taking his leave with any sort of etiquette, he said, "If you can make it to headquarters by the deadline, I'll tell you," and left.

◇ ◇ ◇

Like any normal high school student (or perhaps not), Miyuki spent the first day of winter break doing her homework, and it was shortly after she'd finished eating lunch that an unexpected visitor arrived to call upon her.

"It's been a while, Miyuki. You look quite well."

"You haven't changed a bit, Yuuka. Please, come in."

The guest who sat across from Miyuki in her living room was named Yuuka Tsukuba. She was the oldest daughter of the Tsukuba family, a branch family of the Yotsuba, and one of the candidates to become the next family head.

She was twenty-two years old. She was a former vice president of First High's student council and currently a senior at the Magic University. Her straight black hair reached her shoulders, and it was parted on the side such that it revealed her right ear, which was pierced with a glittering stud. Her makeup was perfect, too; she was the very image of a sophisticated college student.

Miyuki and Yuuka's relationship could be summed up with a single word: neutral. And more specifically: *mutual noninterference.* Yuuka neither regarded Miyuki as a rival the way Ayako did, nor was she friendly like Fumiya was, nor was she openly hostile the way the other family head candidate—Katsushige, from the Shibata family—was. In a way, Yuuka was the least likely person to visit Miyuki like this. A less surprising scenario would have been Katsushige arriving uninvited to make some declaration of war.

Nevertheless, Yuuka did not regard Miyuki with any animosity. They were both candidates for leadership of the family. If she was going to come visit, so long as it wasn't at some unearthly hour, there was no reason to turn her away.

"It's been almost a year since the last New Year."

"Yes, it has."

"We both live in Tokyo, but it seems like we don't get many chances to see each other."

"Tokyo's a big place, after all."

"True. You can really feel it in times like these, though. You're a junior at First High, right? And I hear you're the student council president?"

"That's right. You're well-informed."

"Well, it's my alma mater. You're awfully active in the school, too, I hear."

"I know it's not really ideal at this stage to stick out that much, but I feel like stepping back from activities would be rude, somehow, so I end up like this. You'll be graduating soon, right, Yuuka?"

"That's right. But I'm just continuing on into grad school, so..."

"You're not going to go help the family?"

"Seems like they want me to rack up a little more substance. Little late for that."

Minami brought tea as the two conversed innocuously.

The tone was innocuous enough, but the content was actually quite accusing. Yuuka's comment that Miyuki was *awfully active* was clearly implying that Miyuki stood out too much, and Miyuki's reply that she didn't want to step back for fear of being rude was meant to criticize Yuuka's disguising of her abilities during her own high school years.

Thereafter, Miyuki's question about helping the family was a sly way of asking whether Yuuka was going to leak secret Yotsuba technology to the university.

Though she was certainly capable of holding her own in one, this sort of underhanded conversation was not something Miyuki enjoyed. She welcomed the opportunity to start over, which the tea's arrival brought.

As she and Yuuka simultaneously set their cups down on their saucers, Miyuki broached the topic of Yuuka's visit.

"So, Yuuka—what brings you here today?"

Yuuka dropped her roundabout play at the question. "About the upcoming New Year's celebration—would you like to accompany me?"

"…Are you asking me to travel with you from Tokyo to the family home?"

"Yup. I'll have a car, so you should ride with me."

"May I ask your reason for this?"

Miyuki couldn't hide the wariness that welled up within her. It was unavoidable; Yuuka was one of her rivals to take over leadership of the family, and normally they had very little interaction. Apart from being related by blood, they were practically strangers, and Miyuki knew almost nothing about her save her face.

Letting her suspicion show was a rookie negotiation error, but Yuuka gave no evidence that she'd noticed. Miyuki's halo effect led

most people to underestimate her. Despite her superb skill with magic and her rare beauty, Miyuki was still only sixteen years old, six years younger than Yuuka—but Yuuka was perfectly aware that her excellence was far from superficial and so cleanly evaded this logic trap.

"My reason? Well…do I *have* to say?" Yuuka asked with coquettishly upturned eyes. She was met only by a cold gaze from her conversation partner. "Oh, fine," she said, quickly abandoning the joke, evidently not seriously attempting any deception. "The reason is that I've lost my bodyguard."

"Lost? I thought you had a Guardian—"

Miyuki was about to get up from the sofa, but Yuuka closed her eyes and shook her head rapidly, stopping her. "Not anymore. Vanished before my very eyes. I guess *died* is a better word."

Miyuki covered her mouth with her hand briefly, just long enough to blink.

She was ashamed at her ignorance. She ought to have known that *lost* was a euphemism for *killed*.

Yuuka was a magician of the Yotsuba and an adult in her own right. Given her magical specialization, she wasn't likely to be sent on dangerous missions, but it certainly wasn't impossible. Which meant that the probability of her Guardian being killed in the line of duty was not zero.

And Yuuka specialized in mental interference magic. It was entirely plausible that someone who knew her abilities would target her for her *genetic* qualities.

"I'm…so sorry for your loss."

Yuuka shook her head again at the words Miyuki offered with a bow. "Condolences aren't right for this. Her job was to protect me with her life, and she fulfilled her duty. She'll never again have to fear putting herself in danger for my sake. If there is an afterlife, I know she's breathing a sigh of relief there at no longer being led around by a selfish little brat."

Yuuka's frankness sat poorly with Miyuki.

"Even as a joke, that seems a bit thoughtless to say of one who died protecting you, just because they happened to serve as a Guardian."

Yuuka blinked several times at the unexpected statement. "...That's right, your Guardian is your older brother, isn't it? I apologize if I put unpleasant thoughts in your mind."

Superficially, Yuuka's apology seemed sincere, but something else crept into the edges of her words, and Miyuki found herself unable to take the contrition at face value. "That's not something that's only between my brother and me. Setting aside Fumiya, who doesn't formally have a Guardian, Katsushige values Kotona very highly, doesn't he?"

Kotona Tsutsumi was Katsushige Shibata's Guardian, and it was clear that she was very precious to him. But the example was a poor one. Despite Miyuki's intention to cite that fact to provoke some reflection on Yuuka's part, she merely chuckled quietly instead. "Katsushige and Kotona? Well...you know how they are."

Miyuki stared dumbfounded at Yuuka as she continued to giggle with her head turned askance. Miyuki couldn't deny her own misstep.

"Even if my brother and I don't accompany you, surely you'll be able to quickly arrange for a bodyguard, won't you? Unlike us, you're affiliated with the Tsukuba family."

Yuuka stopped laughing and gave Miyuki a sidelong glance. "True, but..." she started, re-squaring herself to Miyuki, "there aren't many who are as capable as your brother...and it wouldn't be a bad arrangement for you two, either, would it? You can't take a taxi to the main house, and Tatsuya only has a motorcycle license, right?"

It was true that she couldn't very well direct a cabdriver to the headquarters of the Yotsuba clan, which didn't appear on any maps, and she had enough stuff she needed to bring with her that going by motorcycle wasn't practical.

But none of that had ever been a problem. "All I need to do is call in advance, and the family will send someone to pick me up from the train station. That's what I did last year, and that's what I plan to do this year."

Miyuki was a candidate to become the family's next leader, and moreover, she was the niece of the current head. She was certainly important enough to merit VIP treatment in the form of a ride from the station.

"Isn't that what you yourself did last year, too, Yuuka?"

Automotive engineering had already achieved near-ubiquitous semiautomatic driving. Even without the support of automated traffic management, the burden on the driver was far less than it had been in the previous century.

That said, the driving of a motor vehicle was not yet completely effortless. The two hours it took to drive from Tokyo to the Yotsuba headquarters could be done nonstop, but if she could arrange to be picked up, it would be far easier to take a cabinet to the nearest station and switch to a car from there. There was no reason for her to drive herself.

"I don't particularly mind if you do that, but I really do think you should reconsider."

"Why is that? It didn't cause any inconvenience before."

"Not last year, no. However, this year, I do recommend reconsidering. I can't say why, though."

If Yuuka couldn't say why, that meant it wasn't some vague concern but rather something very specific.

"What do you know, Yuuka?"

"I can't say."

"…Why can't I do the same thing I did last year? What benefit is there to traveling with you?"

"I can't say." Yuuka met Miyuki's serious gaze with perfectly feigned innocence.

"I see." Miyuki stopped pushing, but not because she had lost her nerve. She simply didn't have any way to force Yuuka to give up any information.

Not even magic.

Yotsuba magicians were divided into two types: those who

specialized in mental interference magic, and those who specialized in extremely powerful forms of unique magic. As a magician, both categories applied to Miyuki, who practiced a very powerful, unique form of mental interference magic. Yuuka, meanwhile, practiced the archetypical form of mental interference magic.

If it came down to a fight between the two, Yuuka would be far superior at extracting information with a psychological suggestion. Without becoming openly hostile, Miyuki had no way to force her to divulge whatever she was hiding.

"I will inform you of my decision after I have discussed the matter with my brother."

"Oh? Well, I'll hope for a favorable answer. For both our sakes." Yuuka stood. As Minami held the front door open in the entryway, Yuuka offered, "The tea was delicious," and then, as Miyuki watched her go, left the Shiba house with a nonchalant, "See ya round."

"Yuuka said all that?" After returning home, Tatsuya took in his sister's report of Yuuka's visit, then mulled it over. Naturally, with only that much information, he was also unable to determine the truth of what Yuuka—and by extension, the entire Tsukuba clan—wanted. But he was certain that Yuuka's request and Mitsugu's unreasonable demand were somehow related. "And you're certain she wasn't just being vague about it? She definitely knew something but said she couldn't say what it was?"

"Yes. It seemed like she wasn't trying to hide the fact that she knew something."

Which meant that there was something to know. That wasn't even a deduction; it was an established fact. And it wasn't about the New Year's celebration itself but rather something between their home and Yotsuba headquarters.

There was also some degree of possibility that Yuuka was trying to sow uncertainty enough to stop Tatsuya and Miyuki from attending the celebration entirely. But—

It probably means that an attack on us is being planned.

That seemed the likeliest possibility, taking Mitsugu's *intimidation* into account.

But where will they attack? And more important, who's the target? Is it Miyuki? Or could it be me?

If Tatsuya was the target, there were any number of leads to consider. Any time he did a black op, he did his very best to make sure his identity wasn't revealed. He was sure he hadn't left any witnesses. But if he'd made some mistake and revealed an operation as his doing, there could certainly be an organization or two somewhere out there willing to disregard the risk in order to exact retribution.

But even supposing a revenge plot from some criminal organization, why would they go to all the trouble of choosing this particular moment? It didn't make sense. Choosing a place with fewer witnesses would have the opposite of the desired effect when the target was a magician; because the targeted party would have the excuse of self-defense when counterattacking with magic, it made it that much riskier to attack at all.

On the other hand, if the target was Miyuki, their antagonist's aims were quickly narrowed down—it would involve the succession of the Yotsuba clan's leadership. It seemed to Tatsuya that there was little to be gained in taking leadership at the expense of others. If Miyuki wanted to recuse herself, he certainly wouldn't stop her. To his eye, the other candidates for the position weren't especially enthusiastic about it. It was the older generation that cared so much.

But that didn't mean that none of the candidates would be willing to take drastic action, given their elders' feelings. The route from the train station to the family headquarters ran through the Yotsubas' core land holdings, which meant it was the home field for the branch families as well. It was the perfect place for deniability.

If Miyuki was the target, they ought to take Yuuka up on her offer. Having her with them might convince any attackers to cancel their operation, and in case they really were attacked, it would make the Tsukuba clan their ally.

If Tatsuya was the target, however, getting Yuuka involved would only weaken their position. Although the invitation to travel together had come from her, the fact that she'd gotten mixed up in an attack at all might well be weighted more heavily.

And even if it wasn't and they accepted Yuuka's proposal, they might then be forced into making a concession of some kind. By traveling with them, Yuuka might be forcing the hand of the person directing the attack. But that still left Tatsuya and Miyuki responsible for getting Yuuka involved. Either way, the one who stood to gain was Yuuka. Even if Miyuki saw no merit in the position of family head, owing a debt to someone very likely to become family head herself had obvious downsides.

"...Let's refuse," Tatsuya said after a length of silent rumination. He could still hear the voice in his mind telling him that it would be better to take Yuuka up on her offer. His intuition whispered that they ought to travel with her, but the situation was too murky, and after considering the various costs and benefits, he had decided that the costs were too high.

"I understand. I'll let Yuuka know, then." Miyuki bowed to her brother and went upstairs to make the call from the visiphone in her bedroom rather than the big display in the living room.

◇ ◇ ◇

"...I'm sorry. You went to all the trouble of coming to invite us in person."

"I'm sorry, too, but don't worry about it. It was rather sudden, after all."

"My sincere apologies."

"It's fine! But if you change your mind, call me anytime. *Any*time, you understand?"

"Yes. *Thank you so much.*"

"Bye, now. Good luck. I'll be *waiting* for you."

Yuuka replaced the visiphone on the table and reclined luxuriously on her own living room sofa, stretching her legs out as she did so. It was a bit of an unseemly pose for a young lady, but at the moment, she lived alone in her condo. There was neither servants haranguing her about her poor manners, nor her mother, who was overfond of lectures.

Until she'd turned twenty, her mother and the housekeeper had taken turns staying here, but that had stopped upon her reaching the age of maturity. So far as Yuuka could manage, she'd packed twenty years of freedom into the past two years. It was only after the loss of her Guardian, who'd never spoken a word against Yuuka's private life, that Yuuka began to suspect that a life lived entirely selfishly might not be an unmitigated good.

Staying in her relaxed position, she mulled over Miyuki's response.

She'd expected to be turned down. In fact, if they'd taken her up on it with the amount of information she'd given them, Yuuka would have felt her fun to be a little bit spoiled. In that unlikely event, Yuuka might have demanded to be named the next family head on the grounds that Miyuki had been so easily taken in by a ruse.

Not that Yuuka particularly wanted the position, though.

The fact that there were multiple candidates in the first place was solely for the sake of appearances. If the Yotsuba rule that the family head must always be the most powerful magician was faithfully followed, then the next head would undoubtedly be Miyuki Shiba. There were no magicians greater than her within the Yotsuba. Even including the current head, Maya, the most powerful magician in the family was Miyuki. Or at least, the Tsukuba family acknowledged as much.

Yuuka—or rather, the Tsukuba family as a whole—had decided to back Miyuki as their choice for successor two years earlier. Yuuka not becoming the head herself was the precondition for her release from the tiresome observation she'd lived under. The only reason she hadn't withdrawn from formal consideration was that her candidacy was still useful as a bargaining chip in ongoing negotiations with the other branch families.

"And Miyuki has *that* 'brother' of hers…"

Yuuka knew what had "happened" around Tsushima and the southern tip of the Korean Peninsula on October 31 of the previous year. And she also knew what had happened in August, four years earlier, in Okinawa.

"I honestly don't think I could take Miyuki on by herself, but with that human weapon on her side? That's dirty pool."

Yuuka didn't drink, but in times like this, she found herself wishing she did. Ever since the creation of some terrible memories after an impulsive experiment with wine (fortunately, advancements in medication quickly cured the hangover) she'd never touched the stuff.

She settled for the appearance instead, pouring some rosehip tea into a glass cup and then holding it aloft to appreciate its color as she spoke to herself. "Still…moving against Tatsuya isn't a sane thing to do. There's no guarantee he'll stay well-behaved. Why are Grandfather Shibata, Uncle Kuroba, and Uncle Shizuka so determined to have him as an enemy? It seems to me that Tatsuya's crucial to the Yotsubas' military power…"

Tipping the glass teacup slightly, Yuuka frowned. It was still too hot, and looking closely at the color, she saw she'd over-steeped it. "And it's not just my uncles… Even the servants of the main house seem to think Tatsuya's somehow illegitimate. What's the point of them rubbing it in his face like that?"

She took a sip of the tea. She didn't frown this time, being well used to its tartness. "And Mother refuses to tell me why it is that Tatsuya just accepts such treatment… Is there some deeper connection here that I don't know about?"

Yuuka set down the half-full teacup and stood. She headed for the bathroom, while behind her a HAR manipulator arm picked up the teacup and carried it to the kitchen.

If Miyuki was named as the next family head at the upcoming New Year's celebration, Yuuka was silently certain that whatever the reason for Tatsuya's contemptuous treatment, it would come to light.

After Yuuka's call, Miyuki had placed a call to the main house and requested an escort come to pick her up at the station on December 29. When her presence was required at a New Year's celebration, normally arriving on the thirty-first would give her enough time to prepare, but the reason she was arriving on the twenty-ninth was the complications she was certain would arise.

The butler who answered the phone, Obara, was a former traffic-control police officer and the person who normally handled arrangements like this.

After her call to Obara, arrangements were made for a car to pick them up from the station at 1:00 PM. There wasn't any particular need for secrecy, in this case. Quite the contrary—in order to avoid any bungling of Miyuki's arrival time, the entire staff of the main house would be informed.

Katsushige Shibata had joined the staff of the Ministry of Defense just this year. There were periodic compulsory vacation days, but the duties were mostly regular, although unlike school, there was no long winter break. He had just arrived home from another day of work packed full of the type of tasks given to junior staff members, which one, if they were being uncharitable, might call *menial*.

Then, as though it had been waiting for that very moment to pounce, his visiphone rang.

"Mr. Katsushige, I'm happy to—" began Kotona, having met him in his apartment's entryway.

"No, I'll get it," he said, stopping her from returning to the living room and instead himself answering the call on a terminal set into the wall.

Appearing on the display was his father, the head of the Shibata family—one of the Yotsubas' branch families—whom Katsushige had met just three days earlier.

"Father. What is it?"

"Ah, Katsushige. You're home?"

"Yes, I just got home."

"I see. Well, have a seat," Osamu said from the other side of the screen.

Ah, so this is going to take a while, Katsushige realized and sat down on the sofa across from the display.

The mass-produced sofa set was a bit cramped for his five-foot-eleven, 175-pound frame, which itself seemed somewhat wasted on an office job. But Katsushige was used to this and adroitly fit his long legs in the space between the sofa and its matching coffee table, composing himself there.

"So, Katsushige, how's work going?"

"I'm still the new guy, so... And didn't you ask me the same question three days ago?"

"Hmph. Did I...?" Katsushige's father had a military disposition, and it was rare to see him stumble over his words like this. Whatever he had called to say, he clearly didn't want to say it.

So Katsushige decided to broach the subject himself. "Father, is this about the upcoming New Year's celebration?" In three more days, they'd be face-to-face, but his father had gone to the trouble of calling. Given the circumstances, Katsushige couldn't think of anything else it could be.

"Yes. Just recently, Miyuki Shiba contacted Obara. Evidently she intends to arrive at the main house on the twenty-ninth."

"Miyuki's coming on the twenty-ninth, too?"

The Ministry of Defense—along with the rest of the central government—did not have a New Year's holiday. A certain number of staff members were always kept in the office in case of unexpected circumstances. And with the constant outbreaks of war in the world, the Ministry of Defense in particular was a year-round operation. But Katsushige the rookie had been given the traditional time off beginning December 29.

"Okay, what of it, then?" Katsushige asked confusedly, the image of his *young relative's* inhumanly fine features appearing in his mind. Given that attendance at the New Year's celebration was mandatory for all candidates for family head, he didn't see what was particularly odd about her plans. He couldn't understand why his father would go to all the trouble to call him over the girl's attendance.

"Katsushige."

"Yes, sir…?" He felt increasing confusion at his father's repetition of his name, but such trivial concerns were blown away by the impact of the words that followed.

"You must not allow Miyuki to attend the celebration."

Katsushige fell silent. It wasn't that he was at a loss for words but rather that so many questions rose up within him that he didn't know which one to ask first.

He finally chose an obvious one with a high degree of usefulness: "Can I ask the reason?"

"Maya intends to name Miyuki as the next family head at the celebration."

"I see. That's unfortunate," Katsushige answered, mildly surprised at how little this revelation shocked him.

Miyuki was a talented magician, and she excelled at the mental interference magic that was the Yotsuba family's specialty. Katsushige was well aware that she was the most powerful of all the candidates.

But even if aptitude in mental interference magic was an important quality for a candidate, it wasn't an absolute requirement. While the previous head, Eisaku, and the one before him, Genzou, had both been mental interference magicians, the current head was Maya, who had no ability in this particular school of magic—particularly when compared to her sister Miya, who specialized in mental structure interference. And when it came to direct combat magic, Katsushige felt that his ability outstripped Miyuki's.

Katsushige had thought that his odds of becoming the next family head were, at least, not bad. But the fact that he wasn't terribly surprised to hear otherwise meant something. *I suppose I already knew, at some level, that Miyuki was the better* Yotsuba *magician.*

"Father, are you worried about me? Because I'm fine. I'm an adult, you know. I'm perfectly capable of wishing her well." It didn't take much effort for Katsushige to summon a smile to his face.

"*That is not the problem,*" came a sharp rebuttal from his father, followed by a shocking statement. "*Maya intends to name Miyuki as the next family head at the celebration, but we must not let that happen.*"

"Father...are you planning to revolt against the family head? Against the Yotsuba?" Katsushige said with a strong note of rebuke in his voice. "On paper, the next head is supposed to be decided after the main family head consults with the branch family heads, but given the influence the main head can bring to bear on the whole family, the naming of the next head is essentially the current head's prerogative. Even if you were able to get all the branch families to agree to back me for the next head, I can't imagine it would be enough to seize control of the entire clan. Surely you must see that, too, Father."

In defiance of his expectations, Osamu nodded. "*I do. And I have no intention of opposing Miyuki's appointment as the next head itself, although I do think you're a more suitable candidate.*"

"...Then what are you getting at?"

"*There is no stopping Miyuki from becoming the next head. But it is still too soon for that.*"

"Just because Miyuki is named as her successor, I can't imagine Ms. Maya retiring any time soon."

"I'm telling you that it's too soon for Miyuki to be named as her successor."

"She's only sixteen years old. It's no surprise she's still a bit green in some areas."

Katsushige didn't understand his father's real motivations. He could understand if the complaint had been that Miyuki was too young to immediately succeed Maya, but what was the problem with her simply being named as the eventual successor?

"I have no issue with Miyuki herself. I'm sure she's a magician worthy of leading the Yotsuba clan."

At Osamu's words, Katsushige grew still more confused. "...So what *do* you have an issue with?"

"The problem is with the boy who's her Guardian."

"Tatsuya? I can see why he might leave something to be desired as a magician overall, but as a combat magician, he's undeniably powerful. And as Taurus Silver, he's significantly improved the Yotsuba clan's financial position. Above all else, as a strategic-class magician, he's become Japan's trump card. Compared to his Material Burst, even Mio Itsuwa's Abyss seems limited, since it's restricted to watery environments."

"Material Burst is precisely the problem. It's too powerful. Working in the Ministry of Defense, you should know better than me that its use off the southern tip of the Korean Peninsula was what pushed us into secret negotiations with the anti-Japanese military forces."

"There have been such activities, yes, but behind that, there's also been an increase in contact working toward a security treaty for Japan. The New Soviet Union is among the nations that have started seeking an alliance with us. The increase in tensions with the USNA is a downside, it's true, but within the ministry, it's accepted that this is outweighed by the restraint it imposes on the nations immediately surrounding us."

"If his value as a political instrument is already that high, then it's that much more important to isolate him from the Yotsuba centers of influence, to preclude the possibility of the family being drawn into political power plays. And to do that, we need a bit more time. If Miyuki is named successor now, it will automatically place him right beside the next head of the family. And for the future of the Yotsuba clan, nothing could be worse."

Osamu's position seemed logical, but Katsushige couldn't help but try to rationalize the visceral aversion he felt to it. "But, Father, why do you—no, not just you—why do the heads of all the branch families want so badly to see Tatsuya eliminated?"

All expression faded from Osamu's face as he attempted to hide how much the question disturbed him. But Katsushige could see that the other side of that expressionlessness was an accumulation of not days' but years' worth of grievances.

"A power so great threatens the very stability of the world. What we are seeking is power that harms no one. We have no wish for power to make the world tremble."

"But that's not Tatsuya's responsibility, is it?"

"We have no intention of shouldering the responsibility for him. What we see as our responsibility is to seal that boy and his magic away."

Katsushige realized that trying to persuade his father otherwise was folly. He decided instead to try and keep the danger to his fellow family members as low as possible. "What should I do, then?"

"The Mashiba and Shizuka families are already moving against him."

"Is Mr. Kuroba not taking any action?" Katsushige's surprise motivated the question. Neither the Mashiba nor Shizuka families specialized in covert operations. They were roughly as capable of it as any of the other Ten Master Clans, but it was the Kuroba family who were the espionage specialists of the Yotsuba as a whole. For an operation requiring as much subtlety as this one, it would be very strange for the Kuroba family not to be involved.

"The Kuroba have already agreed to the necessity of Tatsuya Shiba's removal. But because Mr. Kuroba's children have been manipulated by

Tatsuya into having a favorable view of him, he's said they're holding back from taking immediate action."

His father's explanation made it clear that the branch families were united in this purpose but included the fact that the family most likely to be effective in the operation was dropping out of actual participation. The entire situation made Katsushige anxious about the future, and he quickly decided that he would do the most good by trying to minimize harm. To do so, he needed to know more about their preparations.

"I see. So what, specifically, are you planning to do?" he asked.

"There's no need to harm Miyuki. The goal is to simply delay her. Ensuring she doesn't arrive by New Year's Day will be sufficient." Katsushige felt marginally relieved upon hearing this surprisingly peaceful tactic. *"Your role will come on December thirty-first. So long as we successfully delay her until then, all will be well. If Mashiba and Shizuka fail, you'll be the last line of defense."*

"Please give me as much detail as you can. If you know them, please include the Mashiba and Shizuka operational plans, as well."

In response to his son's question, all the machinations' details poured from Osamu's mouth.

Thursday, December 27, evening.

At the National Defense Force's Matsumoto Base, First Lieutenant Yaguchi collapsed onto his bed.

As an officer, he had been trained to be a constant example to enlisted soldiers, right down to his personal grooming, and as such, he'd managed to at least keep showering—but beyond that, Yaguchi had nothing left to give.

It was an incident that led to the dismissal of a commanding officer he deeply respected that had fueled Yaguchi's descent into apathy.

Until that incident, Lieutenant Yaguchi had been a member of the

Anti–Great Asian Alliance unit. Led by Colonel Sakai, the fervently patriotic unit kept to the highest standards of conduct regardless of how coldly the rest of the military treated them, openly objecting to the danger that they saw in compromising with the Alliance and the nation behind it. After the Scorching Halloween offered a rare opportunity, and the top brass opted instead to hasten a cease-fire, Colonel Sakai refused to dirty his hands with it, instead continuing to protest.

Finally, just when others in the National Defense Force began to come around, the other shoe dropped: The existence of Parasidolls was revealed to the public, along with suspicions that minors—high school students—had been used as experimental subjects.

But the leak was all part of the Kudo family's plan. Colonel Sakai and his confederates had clearly been set up, and so it was that the man at the heart of the Anti–Great Asian Alliance unit was sent to a military prison. The maximum sentence was five years, but even once it was served, he wouldn't be allowed to return to military service. It was even doubtful whether he would leave prison alive. Many of the brass who'd backed him had died mysterious deaths even before beginning their sentences.

Because of his youth and his low rank, Lieutenant Yaguchi had avoided being implicated. At the time, it was significant that he had not been present at the scene. He'd been transferred to Matsumoto Base from his previous posting as a test pilot for a special mobile infantry unit that was evaluating mechanized armor—essentially powered suits—for practical deployment. It wasn't a demotion, though, as his training as an officer had thoroughly taught him the value of ordinary military service, so Yaguchi didn't feel he'd been relegated to the hinterlands at all.

And so he assiduously participated in each drill and exercise, every inch the exemplary soldier, determined not to further damage the reputations of his former superiors, the hard-liners, who'd been so unfairly accused.

Yaguchi was tired. An outside observer would have said he was pushing himself too hard. Despite his total loss of motivation, he continued to force his body to move. He was mentally depleted, as well—which explained why he'd lent his ear to a strange whisper that day.

There should have been no one in the room except for him. He bolted upright from where he lay in his bed. Exhausted or not, his training had sharpened his hearing to a perfect edge. "Who's there?!" he called.

"It was the Yotsuba of the Ten Master Clans who arranged the downfall of Colonel Sakai and the rest of the Anti–Great Asian Alliance hard-liners." The strangely withered voice came from a corner of the room. It was a lifeless sound, like it could have easily been mistaken for the winter wind blowing through a stand of bare trees.

"…Is that true? Who are you anyway? What proof of that do you have?"

"I cannot show you any proof, but it is true."

Yaguchi's immediate suspicion wasn't just the result of his military training; it was the natural human reaction. "But why would one of the Ten Master Clans do that? Why would the Yotsuba?"

But despite his misgivings, what the voice told him next was something Lieutenant Yaguchi couldn't ignore: *"The figure who directed the Yotsuba against Colonel Sakai is not yet satisfied."*

As Yaguchi fixed his gaze in the direction of the voice, he could make out a humanoid shadow faintly haunting that corner of the room. That was where the cold, withered sound was coming from.

"The figure…? Who?! Who was it who brought down the colonel?!" Yaguchi hissed, keeping his voice low to avoid alerting anyone in the adjoining rooms.

But the answer was not forthcoming; the voice was sticking to its own priorities. *"They plan to assassinate all of the hard-liners, beginning with Colonel Sakai."*

Yaguchi was starting to suspect it of being a recorded message, but he was soon disabused of that notion. "That's absurd. Military prisons are strictly isolated with heavy security. It would be like trying to breach the prime minister's residence. It's impossible to penetrate," he objected, almost in spite of himself.

"*It's not impossible for the Yotsuba,*" said the voice. "*The prison's walls, bars, and security systems will do nothing against Yotsuba magic. It will take more than that to prevent the assassination.*"

Before Yaguchi could respond, the voice continued. "*At one PM on December twenty-ninth, a Yotsuba VIP will arrive at Kobuchisawa Station with a minimal security detail. She will then transfer to a car, which will take her to a hot spring owned by the Yotsuba, where she plans to stay.*"

"...What are you trying to say?"

"*The VIP is a young woman. A girl.*" It was impossible to tell whether the voice said this in answer to Yaguchi's question or to prepare him for what came next. "*The Yotsuba family cannot risk losing this girl. If she is taken captive, she can be traded for the release of Colonel Sakai.*"

"That's not..." ...*Possible*—but Yaguchi didn't finish. Despite being falsely accused, Sakai had been officially convicted by a military court, then imprisoned. Yaguchi didn't think that the Yotsuba had the influence to overturn Sakai's sentence. Or rather, he didn't *want* to think that could be true.

"*It is possible.*"

Yaguchi couldn't bring himself to refute this. He'd pushed the voice to say it was possible. He'd heard the words.

"But taking her as a hostage? How...?" He was already on board with the mysterious shadow's plan. He was forced to admit that his willingness to dirty his hands with this illegal scheme showed just how much he wanted to help the colonel and the other hard-liners. "...I don't have any way to do that!"

"*There is a detention camp for enhanced psychics here.*"

"What?! Don't tell me you want to use them to..."

Enhanced psychics were developed during the Twenty Years' Global War Outbreak as part of ongoing magical research in order to quickly wring improved abilities out of subjects. After the war, these psychics—the products of their nations' darkest impulses—were locked away in various research facilities because of the danger their abilities posed. One such facility was not far from Matsumoto Base, where physically enhanced psychics who were classified as relatively low risk were kept.

"Enhanced psychics have a jealousy of the Ten Master Clans that borders on a grudge. With our operation striking at the Yotsuba, it will be simple to secure their cooperation."

Yaguchi slumped and shook his head at the shadow's certainty. "No, it's not possible. My clearance isn't even close to what I'd need to get into the research facility."

"We will provide that solution. Of course, it won't be a legitimate order."

"…So you're telling me to become a criminal?" Resentment colored Yaguchi's voice—but the moment he hadn't instantly rejected illegal methods, he'd chosen his path.

"Colonel Sakai's conviction itself was obtained illegally. If you can secure the target, the success of our extralegal measures becomes possible." In other words, not only would he rescue Colonel Sakai, but Yaguchi's crimes themselves would be erased. *"We will merely be untangling this perversion of law and restoring true justice. Even if it is a crime, it is not a sin."*

"…Okay. What should I do?"

Although it had no form—no eyes, nose, or mouth—Yaguchi could feel the shadowy form grin.

Around the same time that Lieutenant Yaguchi was making up his mind to break military law at Matsumoto Base, that same shadow appeared at the National Defense Force's Uji Resupply Base Number Two, revealing itself to the leader of the Great Asian Alliance's reconciliation faction, Captain Hatae.

After October, Hatae had been charged with deliberately allowing foreign magicians into the base, but after it was determined that he had been influenced by mental interference magic, his charges had been reduced. For the charge of commandeering a combat vehicle without orders from the base commander, his pay was docked for six months. It was an economically severe punishment, but some would say it was quite generous that he hadn't been demoted, and Hatae himself would have agreed.

Of course, that didn't change his stance. Despite the cessation of hostilities, the Great Asian Alliance was still regarded as an enemy, and Hatae had been warned by both his peers and his superiors that supporting any of its citizens too much would adversely affect his position in the military. And yet, he persisted.

He had no compunctions about being a martyr, but he could sense that his situation was worsening by the day. Even if he wasn't in danger of being purged, the despair that came with the slow death of being put out to pasture weighed heavily upon him.

And then the shadow appeared.

"An illusory projection, huh?" Hatae was more conversant in magic than Lieutenant Yaguchi of Matsumoto Base, which let him immediately identify the nature of the apparition. But knowing what it was didn't tell him anything about the magician casting it. By that measure, there was little difference between him and Yaguchi. "Whose magician are you? Which country?"

"I work for the Yotsuba, who recently attacked this base."

The shadow didn't answer his question, but Hatae didn't mind—he hadn't expected it to. If it had been interested in sharing details, it wouldn't have appeared as a faceless shadow. "I figured that much," he responded.

Hatae had an inkling that the Yotsuba had been involved. The infiltrators had clearly been using modern magic. It was hard to imagine modern magicians bold enough to attack a military base coming from anywhere but the Yotsuba clan. But he couldn't dismiss what the shadow said next:

"Even now, the Yotsuba continue to hunt down anyone connected with the Great Asian Alliance."

"They're still going after my comrades?! Damn those dogs!"

"How odd. I'd have thought you'd be more concerned that you yourself are still a target."

Hatae flinched but quickly recovered his composure. "I may have been manipulated, but I still attempted insurrection. I'm prepared for my fate."

"No honorable end is coming for you. As a traitor, the only death awaiting you is one marred by shame."

"Nrgh…!"

"You committed the sad, small treachery of becoming a tool in the hands of a foreign nation's magicians, despite being an officer in the National Defense Force. Your family must be very ashamed indeed."

"Then—!"

"Ending your own life now would change nothing. You would simply be seen as someone who took refuge in death, unable to bear the shame of your treachery. If you were going to die, you would have had to do so immediately after the incident. If you'd killed yourself then, you'd have been buried as a soldier who'd atoned for his sins via honorable death. But the window for that has long since closed."

"So what should I do?!" Hatae's face showed his desperation. The accusations of the shadow had destroyed all rational thought within him.

"You live on. Staying alive gives you the chance to redeem yourself."

"But how?!"

The shadow grinned. But the expressionless, faceless grin did not seem directed at Hatae. *"On the morning of December thirtieth, three days from today, the very same magician that attacked this base will make contact with the Yotsuba clan."*

"What?"

"The purpose of the contact is resupply and the transmission of new orders. The orders will be to resume the extermination of the Great Asian Alliance reconciliation faction."

"What...are you asking me to do?" asked Hatae through gritted teeth. He was starting to guess at what the shadow's intent might be. "Are you asking me to assassinate that magician?"

"This is merely the first step. If you want to stay alive, you will have to fight for it. If you don't strike back, you will be killed."

"So my only choice is to lower myself to assassination?!"

"I leave that decision entirely to you, Captain Hatae."

Hatae could no longer speak past his clenched jaw.

"One might call you fortunate. You have many who could be called allies. Those ancient magician friends of yours—I'm sure they'll be only too happy to help you."

The shadow disappeared without waiting for Hatae to reply. Being a mere projection, it left behind no trace that it had ever existed in the first place.

[3]

Saturday, December 29: The day when Tatsuya—and, more importantly, Miyuki—would go to the Yotsuba headquarters had arrived.

After finishing an early lunch, Tatsuya, Miyuki, and Minami headed out shortly before noon.

The village where the Yotsuba headquarters was situated hadn't allocated the residence a formal address, so unfortunately, they couldn't use automated luggage delivery. This meant that they had to carry a considerable amount with them, but as they only had to walk to the cabinet station, it was doable; most of the luggage was merely clothing and toiletries and therefore wasn't particularly heavy—just bulky. Especially because the formal kimono that Miyuki would wear on-site was provided by the household every year.

It took just shy of an hour to travel from their home to their destination of Kobuchisawa Station. They encountered no mishaps and arrived at the station right on time.

Tatsuya hadn't forgotten about Mitsugu Kuroba's demand, which was essentially an attack plan, but had decided that there was almost no chance that they would commit what would amount to an act of terrorism on the public transit system. It wasn't the Yotsuba style to openly make an enemy of the government. If there was going to be an attack, Tatsuya thought, it would come after they'd left the station.

The car sent to pick them up was already waiting. Tatsuya recognized the driver, while Minami, who had worked at the main house herself up until the previous year, seemed to have some deeper acquaintance with him. He greeted her with a smile and a short exchange—although when he looked back to Tatsuya, his face became blank again, as though he was regarding the luggage.

After he loaded the suitcases in the trunk, Tatsuya led Miyuki into the car, since if she had seen the way the driver was looking at him, it would've caused needless hassle. For his part, Tatsuya simply wished the driver had been willing to keep up a bit more of an act in order to avoid pointless trouble, but any driver employed by Obara was likely to have been chosen for his skills rather than any propensity to dole out social niceties. Those skills wouldn't just be at driving, either—the man could undoubtedly handle himself in a fight, so a certain lack of grace was to be forgiven.

There was another reason Tatsuya hurried Miyuki into the vehicle. As he'd expected, they were being watched—and it felt less like a watchful gaze over their party and more like the car itself was being surveilled.

If they had an asset within Yotsuba headquarters, or some other source of intelligence, it was entirely possible that they knew this car had been sent specifically to pick up Miyuki. Tatsuya had a hard time believing that they would really go so far, but whatever the reality was, his guess wouldn't change it.

However, there were fewer eyes on them than he'd anticipated, which concerned him. It gave him the impression that their destination was known and an ambush was already lying in wait for them. If information had leaked, it wasn't impossible.

And as it stood, there wasn't any sign of imminent movement against them. It was illegal to employ magic for purposes other than self-defense, so since all they were doing was watching, he couldn't use magic to dispose of them—nor could he do so nonmagically. The only course of action available was to get in the car and get moving as quickly as possible.

Minami ended up sitting in the front passenger seat. It had the best visibility, but when Tatsuya tried to get her to surrender it, Minami—somewhat apologetically—refused to budge, so he ended up keeping watch from the back seat.

He noticed movement as soon as they left town: A suspicious vehicle tripped Tatsuya's warning net.

Miyuki noticed her brother's guard go up even before he had a chance to say anything—normally their close communication sped things up, but in this case, it introduced a moment of delay.

"Brother, what's…"

"It's an attack!" Even just cutting off her question stole a bit of time. "Grenade rounds—two from the front, one from the rear!"

The target was the car they were all riding in. Minami began casting an anti-penetration and anti-heat barrier, but thanks to the disorder directed at them by *eleven other people*, her magic was incomplete and compromised.

The Cast Jamming effectively blocked Minami's magic by mutual interference.

This was no accident, Tatsuya realized. This sort of coordination couldn't be achieved with a day or two of practice. Creating a resonant state between eleven spell programs was something that had to be carefully calibrated—and therefore was clearly deliberate.

This was a way of using magic without using magic. It was as if the technique were made specifically for people who couldn't use magic, a combat ability made for experimentally strengthened individuals who'd failed to become magicians.

"Minami, cancel your magic!"

"What? Okay!"

Without waiting for her reply, Tatsuya pointed diagonally up with his right hand. On his chest he wore a thought-activated CAD, and on his wrist was another one—a Silver Torus.

The grenade rounds disintegrated in midair, their silenced propulsion units shattering against the surface of the road.

Two, then three more high-explosive rounds followed, only to meet the same fate.

Their car slipped easily past a few small explosions. The fall had triggered the fuses of the high explosives, detonating them—but fortunately, since they were separated from the explosives they'd been meant to trigger, those remained inert.

Tatsuya waved his hand above his head as though swatting away an insect. The magic he activated was Program Dispersion, instantly interfering with the fixed-resonance magic that had been directed at them.

"Head back to town!" Tatsuya ordered the driver, taking no notice of Minami looking downcast and ineffective in the front seat.

But the driver merely glanced in the rearview mirror at a vehicle pursuing them, where a grenade launcher protruded from its window. He neither touched the brake pedal nor made the slightest motion toward the parking brake.

Heedless of Tatsuya's words, he was preparing to force his way through.

"Please, turn the car around!" said Miyuki, echoing her brother's direction.

"Understood!" The driver instantly followed Miyuki's order.

"Minami, watch over Miyuki," Tatsuya said, pulling a pair of heat-resistant, bulletproof sunglasses out of his breast pocket.

"O-okay!"

His features now obscured behind the wraparound sunglasses, Tatsuya spoke to Miyuki next. "Miyuki, I'll see you at the station."

"Brother?!"

Tatsuya opened the window just as the driver sent the car into a spin turn.

Antilock brakes were universally installed in virtually every vehicle by this time, making handbrake drift turns impossible by design, but since the car was equipped with four-wheel steering with a high degree of freedom, a skilled driver could turn the car in such a tight radius that it seemed to be spinning in place. The maneuver had come to be called a *spin turn*.

The moment the car spun, Tatsuya used the centrifugal force of the spin to leap from the back-seat window of the car. A combination of his inertia and leap brought him to the ground, where Tatsuya promptly disintegrated the weapons of the attackers behind the car, preventing any further attacks on the vehicle itself.

He looked over his shoulder and saw the attackers' vehicle in mid-turn as it prepared to pursue Miyuki. Tatsuya targeted its wheels, which promptly fell off, and the air was filled with a high-pitched grinding sound as the vehicle's body scraped against the pavement.

After confirming that his sister's car was headed safely back to town, Tatsuya launched himself at the nearest attacker.

His opponent couldn't have anticipated an attack coming like this, but he was quick to react. He revealed no confusion at the guns that disintegrated. He wore the uniform of a shipping company, and as Tatsuya charged him unarmed, he reached back and produced a hand-to-hand combat knife, with both a wide finger guard and a bladed knuckle-duster.

An enhanced National Defense soldier? No—an artificial psychic!

The man's equipment implied the assumption that he wouldn't be able to rely on firearms during combat. No ordinary soldier or criminal would carry something like this. Considering the deliberately constructed interference magic program from earlier, there was no doubt this man was an artificial psychic—an experimental subject who'd failed to become a magician.

The knife lashed out at him. He could "see" that the high-grade stainless steel blade was electrified. Even before he'd grasped that his opponent was an artificial psychic, Tatsuya had been using Elemental Sight alongside his regular vision. At this rate, even if he deflected the blade, he would take damage from the arcing electric charge stored within—and it wasn't a nonlethal weapon like a stun gun. It would deliver a lethal amount of current.

Instead of barely avoiding the blade, Tatsuya leaped back, opening a large gap.

Sparks flew from the tip of the knife, arcing from the blade up the man's arm. He seemed to be wearing protective gear of some kind, as he gave no sign of being affected by the electricity. He was shocked, though, by something else:

The man froze, realizing that his abilities had betrayed him, his powers having been activated against his will. Instantly, Tatsuya held his palm out toward the man, hammering the consciousness out of him with a pressure wave.

It had been simple enough to make the man's knife discharge on its own. As he'd jumped back, Tatsuya had fired off a carefully constructed magic program that dismantled the magic containing the electrical charge. Modern magic had, after all, arisen from research into psychic abilities. It was common sense to Tatsuya that the two were fundamentally the same thing.

The man wore a construction helmet with a baseball cap–like visor low over his eyes to disguise his face, but it came off when the man fell—revealing the face of a boy perhaps fifteen years old.

Tatsuya didn't have time to look carefully at his face. More enemies were approaching rapidly from both sides. They wore the same shipping company uniforms as the boy, with the same hard hats. It wasn't a stretch to determine they were teammates.

Speed-wise, they were comparable to Erika, the fastest magician he knew. But when it came to their control…

Sloppy, he thought.

Two more psychics were coming at him, slightly offset in timing. If Tatsuya did nothing, the man to his right would make contact first; that was who he moved toward.

He didn't counterattack, though—he only moved past the man.

When he came to a stop with the man behind him, the man was still moving.

The psychic attacking from the left passed by the one coming from the right, and Tatsuya prepared to face him.

The knife came out.

Palm met head.

Tatsuya evaded the knife and maneuvered behind his attacker, rattling his mind with another pressure wave from his palm.

Did I kill him? Tatsuya wondered for an instant at the deeper-than-expected response he felt, but after sensing life signs from the man's collapsed body, Tatsuya turned again to face the other psychic, who had now finally oriented himself.

Acceleration magic was active on the man's body. Tatsuya didn't sense any medium for inertial control. That should have resulted in g-forces beyond what the human body could endure, but the man's combat stance was unaffected.

So he's been physically enhanced. That settles it.

His opponent was a physically enhanced artificial psychic. These magic-wielding soldiers had been developed during the first half of the Twenty Years' War but never completed. Germany had attempted to achieve useful results via genetic manipulation, while Japan had used drugs to make the enhancements.

But it was the thirty-centimeter range limit that had led to physically enhanced artificial psychics being abandoned as a failed project—they could only use weapons that stayed within that range of their body. They couldn't maintain the magic programs necessary for physical effects at distances beyond than that—they could only project diminished psionic information particles, which were incapable of affecting the physical world.

That wasn't entirely meaningless, though. It's impressive that they managed to combine their incomplete magic programs in a way that interfered with other magic. Just goes to show there are clever people everywhere.

All that aside, if these really were the enhanced psychics from those experiments, they had to be over sixty years old. Evidently, their physical enhancements also slowed the aging process.

Those were the kind of thoughts that—if put into words—went through Tatsuya's head in less than a tenth of a second. Meanwhile, he was moving to intercept the strike coming from his magically accelerated opponent, who was coming at him like a cannonball.

Although his speed made him dangerous, his combat technique was unpolished. He looked sloppy, to Tatsuya's eye. Even taking into account that his immediate references of comparison were Yakumo or Yanagi, from a general perspective, the man's technique was objectively lacking.

It wasn't a lack of training. The psychic's speed had been artificially enhanced, but his conscious mind couldn't keep up with his magically improved speed.

Erika was the fastest magician Tatsuya knew, but there were any number of magicians faster than her when it came to simple movement speed. Yanagi was one, as was Kazama. If magical ability came into the equation, Miyuki, Mayumi, and Katsuto could also manage it. Masaki Ichijou, too, probably. But not all of them were at a level where they could use self-acceleration magic during actual combat—not because they didn't need to but because they wouldn't be able to control their own accelerated bodies.

It was only Erika's natural talent that let her keep her balance while controlling both her body and her weapon at such speeds. There was no way to fake her ability—and because Tatsuya was facing exactly such a fake, this would be an easy opponent to handle.

What followed next was only natural:

Tatsuya opened both his palms in preparation. As the psychic swung the knife in a flat arc, Tatsuya caught the man's wrist between his palms.

It almost looked like his opponent himself had wanted to be caught—the scene was practically identical to when Yanagi had fought the No-Head Dragon's generator during the Nines Competition.

Tatsuya killed his own body weight and inertia and, after feinting an arm bar, sprang upward into a head kick. With his weight and inertia canceled, the motion took only an instant.

The unconscious man tumbled to the road, and Tatsuya spun in midair such that the moment he touched down, he was already facing his next target.

With his heightened senses, he counted twenty-eight remaining enemies. Of them, nine were artificial psychics. In addition to the eleven who'd been responsible for the disruption field, there was one more, presumably held in reserve in the car that had pursued them. Nineteen normal humans with no superhuman abilities appeared to be fleeing.

However, Tatsuya did not intend to let a single one of them escape unscathed.

Unfortunately, once the police arrived, Tatsuya had to leave the scene having only taken out twenty of them. He was careful to avoid any police attention, taking his time in making his way back to the station to meet up with Miyuki.

It was past 4:00 PM by the time he returned.

When Miyuki saw him, she flew at him from where she sat in the station's waiting room drinking tea. "You're safe!"

"Sorry to keep you waiting," he offered, patting his sister's head before leading her back into the waiting room where their live-in guard had been left.

"Well done, Minami."

"Not at all. I'm glad you're all right," she said, standing up politely. Tatsuya gestured for her to sit back down, as he did across from her.

Miyuki, needless to say, sat next to her brother. Next to Minami was, instead, three travelers' worth of luggage.

"Where did our car go?"

"I sent it back to the house," Miyuki said. "Given that the attack will certainly have been recorded on traffic cameras, I made sure to specify he take an indirect route. Er... Should I have not done that?" She looked up to him uncertainly.

Tatsuya touched her cheek and smiled reassuringly. "No, you made the right call. Well done, thinking so far ahead."

"Oh, thank you, Brother..." Miyuki flushed and looked down, as Minami regarded the proceedings with a look that said, *Is this really necessary?*

But the moment Tatsuya's eyes moved away from his sister, Minami quickly regained her normal, unassuming expression.

Tatsuya regarded the woman skeptically, having been quick enough to catch the shift in her demeanor. Minami sensibly kept her discomfort to herself.

Fortunately for her, Tatsuya decided against anything as mean-spirited as staring her down and waiting to see how long her bluff would hold out. Instead, he returned his gaze to Miyuki as he removed his hand from her cheek.

"Aw," she murmured, disappointed.

He set her feelings aside for the moment as he directed her to contact the Yotsuba headquarters. "We'll return home for today and try again tomorrow, so have them send another car."

There wasn't any particular problem with arriving at the main house on New Year's Eve. The reason they had tried today was specifically because of the possibility of an accident—or rather, a deliberate interference attempt.

The caution had proved unfortunately warranted, which was all the more reason not to push their luck today.

"Understood," Miyuki said, taking out her portable terminal and opening communications with the main house.

It was the butler Obara who answered. He repeatedly confirmed Miyuki's—and no one else's—safety and well-being, apologized several times for the bungling of her transport, and emphasized that he would immediately send another car.

"...Mr. Obara, I would prefer to return home tonight." Miyuki had finally reached her limit. Her voice wasn't raised in anger; rather, the chill in her tone made it clear to all listening that her mind would not be changed.

"Understood, miss." The voice that came through the receiver was so stiffly proper that one could practically see the man's rigid posture.

Seizing her chance, Miyuki pressed her advantage. "Please inform my aunt that I will deliver a full report upon arriving home."

"Yes, as you wish, miss."

"Also, I'd like a car sent to meet me again tomorrow."

"Certainly. What time should it await your arrival, miss?"

Obara tended toward exaggerated formality, but Tatsuya couldn't remember a time when he'd been quite this stiff. It was off-putting enough that Miyuki hesitated in answering, giving her brother a look that wordlessly asked what to say.

Tatsuya input "10 AM" on his own terminal, then showed it to Miyuki.

"Ten o'clock in the morning, if possible."

"Very well, miss," came Obara's immediate answer.

Miyuki wondered if it really was all right but then quickly decided that it wasn't something she needed to worry about. "All right. We'll expect you tomorrow, then."

"Yes, Ms. Miyuki. Please take care on your way home."

There was something in his tone that Miyuki heard as resentment, but she decided that it was her imagination and ended the call.

Tatsuya, Miyuki, and Minami didn't speak a single word about the incident until they returned home.

Leaving their luggage packed, they gathered in the living room after changing clothes, and only then did the tacit gag order on the topic lift.

Miyuki and Minami brought in black tea and coffee. Miyuki had brewed the coffee for Tatsuya's benefit, while Minami had prepared the tea for herself and Miyuki. Having two people prepare two separate drinks seemed excessive to Tatsuya, but he had decided to keep his opinion to himself on this matter.

"Miyuki, Minami—good work, both of you," he said by way of thanks. He noticed Minami heading to sit at one of the dining table chairs and gestured for her to join Miyuki on the sofa.

"Ah, you can sit here, too, Minami. So…about the people who attacked us today," he began. "The soldiers were physically enhanced artificial psychics—a failed experiment of the National Defense Force."

"Why would the National Defense Force…?" Miyuki's question was about the reason for the attack, but she wasn't disputing her brother. If Tatsuya said they were something, then that something was what Miyuki accepted as absolute truth. "And what are 'physically enhanced artificial psychics' anyway?"

"I don't know the reason. The police arrived as I was neutralizing our attackers, so I didn't have the chance to question them. And as for what they are…"

Tatsuya began to explain the development of artificial psychics. It was a topic he hesitated to broach in front of Minami, herself a second-generation engineered magician, but he ultimately decided it would be more insulting to patronize her by tiptoeing around her feelings.

"…And research into artificial psychics was halted over forty years ago. The experimental subjects are all over sixty years old. I'd heard they were in-house in the former Gunma and Nagano Prefectures, but apparently there were confinement facilities in Suwa and Matsumoto as well."

"They've been confined for over forty years?" murmured Minami. "Just locked away, without being given any duties?" She squeezed her eyes shut to stop the tears. "…But could the test subjects really ever be released from facilities like that? Even supposing they were all volunteers, they're living proof of human experimentation. It might seem to us like after so much time, they should be freed, but the military might still want to hide them from the public—especially the media—forever."

Miyuki's eyes widened in shock at Minami's point. "Could it be that it was a high-level military officer that ordered the attack on us…?"

"No, not possible," Tatsuya said, flatly dismissing her fear. "If this were military espionage, they wouldn't have sent such a mediocre force to face me. Even being willing to throw experimental units at us, they would've employed stronger assets. Most likely ones who were too powerful for even themselves to control and therefore disposable."

In other words, if this really had been the work of the Defense Force brass, they would've planned to let Tatsuya dispose of experimental subjects that had gotten troublesome to handle, even if they couldn't defeat Tatsuya himself. It was an all-too-plausible scenario, and thinking about it was unpleasant, so Miyuki quickly changed the subject.

"Yuuka knew that we were going to be attacked, didn't she?"

"I imagine so. She was probably also thinking that if she'd been with us, we wouldn't be." Tatsuya sipped his coffee blankly. "There's also the issue of Kuroba's warning." He'd told Miyuki and Minami about Mitsugu's attempted intimidation from earlier. "I don't want to believe it, but it's possible that one of the branch families may have been pulling the strings behind today's attack."

"…Is this my fault?" Miyuki asked tremulously.

"No." Tatsuya immediately shook his head. "At least not according to what Kuroba said. The guys that attacked us today weren't only focused on you."

In fact, there wasn't any reason to believe that Miyuki hadn't been the target. Tatsuya got the impression that on the attackers' side, they hadn't had much understanding of who they were attacking—but he had no reason to be so bluntly honest as to say so out loud.

Tatsuya put forth a reasonable deduction based on the background information he already had, plus the events of the day.

"Their motivation is presumably to stop you from attending the New Year's celebration. But they're probably not trying to stop you from inheriting leadership entirely. Rather, this is about delaying the announcement of the next head. If blocking you from becoming family head were the goal, it makes no sense for them to wait until after we departed Kobuchisawa Station. They should've attacked this house while I was away at FLT."

"I…suppose that's true. No, I'm sure you're right, Brother," Miyuki said, trying to convince herself.

Tatsuya felt a pang, but at this moment, easing Miyuki's worries was his top priority. He knew he was only putting off the problem until later, but between that and saddling her with heartache, it was the more constructive option.

"Miyuki, you should call Aunt Maya soon."

"Oh, that's right."

Tatsuya stood and headed for the dining room.

Miyuki stood directly in front of the camera, with Minami behind her to one side, operating the remote control.

On the screen, Maya laughed and accepted Miyuki's apology and said she looked forward to seeing them the next day.

That evening, a young officer stationed at Matsumoto Base died after being involved at an incident near Kobuchisawa Station. In the newspapers the next morning, it was reported that he had wound up in the cross fire between two violent gangs and, in trying to stop their clash, had unfortunately lost his life.

[4]

Sunday, December 30, 8:50 AM.

Just before they left, Tatsuya called ahead to the main house—for his own reasons.

The call was answered by a curt housekeeper, and Tatsuya rather intimidatingly demanded to speak to Obara. Even through the camera, the housekeeper was thoroughly cowed by Tatsuya's gaze and scurried off to fetch Obara.

"Tatsuya, I really cannot have you scaring the maids." Obara served under Aoki, and as one of the butlers who had been told little about him, he treated Tatsuya comparatively well. As the lowest-ranking of the eight butlers who served the main house, he was inclined to treat everyone politely, and perhaps his former career as a traffic-control police officer made him averse to acting high and mighty with any citizen.

Nevertheless, his every word and action made it clear that he considered Tatsuya beneath him.

"This is an urgent matter." Ordinarily, Tatsuya preferred to avoid stirring up trouble. However, today he had no time for niceties.

"And just what is this 'urgent matter' of yours?" Obara's face twitched faintly in displeasure.

Tatsuya noticed this, but he ignored it. Besides, the man's mood was only going to get worse because Tatsuya hadn't even gotten to the meat of his request yet. "We'd like to change our travel arrangements. Please have a car meet us at Nagasaka Shiraisawa, at nine fifty."

"Now, wait just a minute! I've already dispatched the driver—this is highly irregular."

"He hasn't left the house yet, has he? This is a simple change of destination and arrival time. I don't mean to be unreasonable."

Obara's frown was a sincere one. *"It isn't a question of whether it's possible or not—this is simply too little notice."*

"And it is necessary, which is why I am asking."

"Tatsuya, it gives me no pleasure to say this, but you are being rather unseemly. At the very least, I would ask that any changes to itinerary come from Ms. Miyuki herself."

"This change does come from Miyuki. Do I need to ask her to call you to confirm this?"

Obara's face flushed red as he reined in his anger. He wasn't able to hide the frustration in his voice, though. *"Understood. Nagasaka Shiraisawa at nine fifty, then."*

Tatsuya had his reasons for waiting until the last possible minute to communicate the change in plans. Obara's reaction was an unavoidable side effect. "Also, please tell only the driver of the change in destination and no one else."

Obara was no fool, though. His irritation vanished, and he immediately grasped the meaning of Tatsuya's pointed suggestion. *"I assume that has something to do with the incident yesterday?"*

Tatsuya was surprised by this, but if he talked any more about it, he risked ruining this little plan. "I'm sure you understand the need for discretion."

"Indeed."

Tatsuya and Obara hung up on each other simultaneously.

◇　◇　◇

Tatsuya had changed their travel plans because the Yotsuba headquarters had a leak. This was neither a suspicion nor speculation on his part; he was certain.

Of the seven historic houses of the Yotsuba clan, one or more members among the Shiiba, Mashiba, Shibata, and Shizuka were trying to delay the designation of the next clan head in order to separate Tatsuya from Miyuki. The interference with her attendance at the New Year's celebration was a means to that end.

Their actions made no sense to Tatsuya, though. It was true that the annual celebration was the only regular event where the main family and branch families were all gathered together in a single location, but attendance was not absolute. In fact, Miyuki skipped it every year, and their father, Tatsuro, wasn't even permitted to enter the main house.

There was nothing special about New Year's Day making it the only day when the entire clan could assemble, nor was there any rule that said the whole clan had to be present for the designation of the successor. The Yotsuba clan didn't boast a particularly long tradition, either. It had only taken its current form under the leadership of Miyuki and Tatsuya's grandfather, Genzou, making Maya only the third-generation head.

The previous clan leader—Maya's uncle, Eisaku—had been the one to name Maya as his successor, and before he did so, it had merely been accepted that either Miya or Maya would assume the role. Maya had assumed leadership per Eisaku's will and not as the result of any clan discussion or council.

So even if Miyuki were somehow prevented from attending the New Year's celebration, it was unlikely that this would delay her being named successor. Tatsuya got the distinct impression that the branch family heads were being deceived.

But no matter how absurd it seemed, given that their attendance had been ordered, Tatsuya and Miyuki had to make every effort to arrive on time. In fact, the very absurdity of the whole situation made Tatsuya even more determined to show up. He couldn't stand not finding out what was behind this elaborate farce.

His ruse of changing the pickup time and location seemed at first to be successful. At the very least, they weren't immediately followed upon leaving the station, the way they had been the previous day. But Tatsuya didn't think their luck would hold all the way to their destination.

"They've found us, eh?" he murmured, sometime after the scenery had shifted from residential construction to rural countryside.

"Are we being followed?" asked Miyuki.

Tatsuya shook his head vaguely. "We have a tail, but it's not a car. A psionic information construct…though not a spirit. Must be a familiar."

Miyuki's face tensed up. In the front passenger's seat, Minami bit her lip nervously.

"A magician from the mainland?" Miyuki asked.

Tatsuya hadn't expected the question. "…No, it's not the type of compound familiar that they'd use. This is a construction of pure thought, without shape or color."

Miyuki flushed slightly at Tatsuya's answer. "Sorry, when I hear the word *familiar*, that's where my mind goes to first…"

"There's no need to apologize. Since last year, you've had a lot of chances to encounter compound familiars, after all." Tatsuya reassured Miyuki with a smile, but his expression soon turned serious. "It took them this long to find us. The enemy can't be too formidable, but we shouldn't let our guard down. They'll be here soon."

"Okay," Miyuki chimed.

"Understood," added Minami, looking over her shoulder from her seat in the front.

Seemingly absorbed in driving, their driver didn't exchange any words with them. However, his shoulders were noticeably tense, and his face was fixed forward, with only his eyes darting here and there.

True to Tatsuya's guess, it wasn't ten minutes before their enemy revealed itself to them.

The first sign was the distinctive sound of a rotor coming from behind them. "A helicopter, huh?"

"Shall we shoot it down?" proposed Miyuki bluntly, already fully prepared for combat.

"No, we can't be the ones to attack. We're still in the range of their psion sensors," Tatsuya cautioned. He said to the driver: "Keep an eye out ahead. They'll probably try to block the road with a larger vehicle."

Behind them, the helicopter closed in. Tatsuya imagined that the reason they were taking their time when they could've easily caught up by now was to apply extra pressure.

They were being driven like prey, which meant there would be an obstacle ahead on the road.

It was an uncomplicated theory, which made it that much more likely to be correct.

"Brakes!" Tatsuya shouted, despite the green light at the intersection ahead. The driver slammed on the brakes as, just ahead, a trailer truck sped into view, ignoring the signal entirely as it came to a stop in the middle of the intersection.

"Minami, as soon as I get out, put up a shield."

"Will do!"

"Brother, what about me?"

"You're backup in case things go bad!"

Just as Tatsuya got out of the car, a unit carrying automatic weapons deployed from the trailer. From the looks of it—

—*Thirty-two shooters. A platoon's worth. Armed with standard automatic weapons, not anti-magician high-powered rifles.*

As the unit started to take up offensive positions, Tatsuya scrutinized their numbers and equipment.

Sixteen magicians. They're keeping their distances and staying hidden. Two in the chopper. Trying to corner us?

It was a larger scale attack than the previous one, with commanders present.

It won't be enough, though.

Half the enemy force stopped and took aim. It was far more firepower than was necessary for a normal individual target. Whoever their enemy was, they clearly knew something about Tatsuya.

…Or was there a limit to the number of troops they could mobilize before?

A barrier materialized in front of Tatsuya.

The machine guns lit up the road with automatic fire.

Minami's barrier stopped every small-caliber, high-velocity round—an unsurprising outcome, given that her shielding magic could stop even high-powered rifles.

Meanwhile, Tatsuya wasn't just evaluating their enemy's combat potential.

Half the remaining force moved to flank them on both sides. At the same time, Tatsuya targeted them with partial disintegration.

Those sixteen targets were protected by some defensive magic. The program seemed to be an individualized barrier cast by one of the hidden magicians, of esoteric Buddhist origins.

Tatsuya's partial disintegration stripped it away easily.

It wasn't the subtle effect of a three-layered spell like Trident. Tatsuya had simply used his overpowering ability to manipulate magic. He had identified that the caster of the protective spell and the target were not closely linked, and this was the result.

Tatsuya immediately followed this with offensive magic. Hit in both shoulders and both thighs, each soldier was immediately neutralized, and they began to lose consciousness from the pain.

"—Damn you, monster!" Familiar cries from the stricken men reached Tatsuya's ears, but he didn't even bother flashing a wry smile.

Tatsuya only had experience with special forces, but he noted that for an ordinary combat unit, they were rather skilled. Nevertheless, it wasn't enough to stop him, much less have a prayer of holding back Miyuki.

Sixteen shooters left. Have to neutralize them first.

Tatsuya took off running.

He was now the hunter.

Tatsuya took down the helicopters, incapacitated the hidden magicians—without particular concern for the fallout—and captured the officer who seemed to be the unit's commander. Unlike the previous day's attackers, retreat was beneath him, although as far as Tatsuya was concerned, capturing the commander gained him nothing, and neither of them particularly wanted to get the police involved, so he would've been just as happy if the commander *had* tried to escape.

He'd quickly determined that questioning the man would be a waste of time. Despite having supplied a chopper and a camouflaged troop transport, the fact that he hadn't equipped his unit with high-powered anti-magician rifles made it clear to Tatsuya that he hadn't been well-briefed on the details of the operation.

In any case, the dismal wreckage of the fight notwithstanding, Tatsuya had managed to deal with the attack quickly and cleanly—but it wasn't as if his side had sustained no losses at all. Their car was broken.

"I am terribly sorry…"

"It wasn't your fault, Minami, so don't worry about it. I didn't plan for this, either."

"That's right. You did your job perfectly, Minami. It's just like my brother says—don't worry about it."

Though Tatsuya and Miyuki were doing their best to comfort Minami, the fact remained that they were stranded.

The car wasn't broken because Miyuki's barrier had been breached but rather because the attackers had used an unexpected weapon:

"I can't believe they had an EMP bomb…"

The portable EMP—electromagnetic pulse—device was currently under development and had an effective range of a mere ten meters. The tradeoff of having such a small range was that it had been miniaturized enough to fit within an ordinary car. It wouldn't have any effect on military vehicles with electromagnetic shielding, but it worked well enough on civilian transport.

All CADs were manufactured to military specifications, so even regular ones were well shielded, but civilian portable terminals were vulnerable to EMP attack.

"Miyuki, how's your terminal?"

"It seems okay."

"Minami?"

"Mine's also working."

Tatsuya's portable terminal appeared to be a standard consumer-grade model, but its internals were identical to those used by the Independent Magic Battalion. Miyuki's terminal had been provided to her directly from the Yotsuba clan, as had Minami's. None of them would be disabled by a pulse from a portable EMP.

But their car was a different story.

"Still…I can't understand why the car they sent from headquarters to pick us up wouldn't have electromagnetic shielding," complained Miyuki, causing their driver to flinch.

Modern cars were rolling chunks of electronics. A strong enough electromagnetic pulse would render one totally useless.

While high-end consumer automobiles were hardened against electromagnetic pulses, evidently this car's shielding was shoddy—either that, or the bomb had been powerful enough to overwhelm consumer-level countermeasures.

"I'm really very sorry. This was my fault, I know…" Minami apologized again, feeling sorry for the driver Miyuki had taken her frustration out on, even if she hadn't directly scolded him.

And Minami wasn't entirely blameless.

The magic she'd used was called Mass Filter. It was an area-effect program that prevented transmission of matter above a given threshold. She'd set it to filter out anything larger than a CO_2 molecule. Unlike vector inversion or kinetic energy neutralization, it was an extremely effective defensive spell that could ward off even poisonous gases, which were dispersed and nondirectional.

However, Mass Filter had absolutely no effect on electromagnetic radiation, nor did it protect against heat or sudden changes in pressure. Minami had had a Vector Inversion Shield queued and ready to cast in case of an explosion, and she'd probably assumed that with Miyuki around, she wouldn't have to worry about heat.

But she had completely overlooked electromagnetic radiation. Minami considered this a serious mistake. If their enemy had attacked with lightning, she wouldn't have had time to defend. No matter how much Tatsuya and Miyuki tried to console her, their reassurances didn't comfort Minami—so it wasn't merely sympathy that caused her to try to cover for the driver.

Discerning her feelings, Tatsuya changed the subject rather than trying to comfort Minami further. "In any case, Miyuki, let's call another car."

"All right." Miyuki also understood why Minami blamed herself. It hadn't been her intention to be hard on either Minami or the driver. She hadn't meant to grumble out loud at all and was very grateful for the opportunity to change the subject.

But she couldn't call the main house—because at that moment, she received another call.

Tatsuya gave her a look that said *go ahead*, so Miyuki took the call.

"Hello, Miyuki."

It was Yuuka Tsukuba's voice on the other end of the line. "Yuuka?"

"That's right. I'm sorry to contact you out of the blue like this."

"What is it?"

"I was wondering if you would do something about the trailer truck blocking the road."

It was indeed a very peculiar request, but as the trailer hadn't been subjected to any attacks, it would be simple to move. Miyuki ended the call and directed the driver to move the trailer out of the intersection.

Despite Miyuki's certainty otherwise, immediately on the other side of the trailer was none other than Yuuka. Before the driver could return from moving the trailer, she quickly pulled through and stopped next to the disabled car. "Get in."

For a moment, even Tatsuya was at a loss for words at her unexplained demand.

Yuuka raised her voice in irritation despite herself. "Hurry! We can't keep the police away much longer!"

Hearing this, Tatsuya took action. "Miyuki, Minami, get in," he commanded as he went for the luggage. "What about our driver?" he asked once he was done getting it all in Yuuka's trunk and slid into the front passenger's seat.

"He'll figure something out," Yuuka said briskly as she fired up her beloved vehicle, as though any longer of an answer would've been a waste of time.

For a while, there was silence in the car. Yuuka was absorbed in driving. In the passenger's seat, Tatsuya listened to his voice communication unit, occasionally pausing to do something with his portable terminal. He seemed to be intercepting radio transmissions of some kind.

Miyuki spoke up. "Er, Yuuka."

"Yes?"

"I believe the main house is in the other direction." Miyuki couldn't hide the mistrust in her voice.

"I'm trying to avoid the police," Yuuka said wryly.

"She's telling the truth, Miyuki," Tatsuya said, pulling his ear from the comms device and looking back over his shoulder to reassure his sister. "The police set up a checkpoint in the direction of the house, but they didn't do one going the other way, for some reason."

Tatsuya had been listening to police chatter. That wasn't something an ordinary consumer terminal could do, but his only *appeared* ordinary—its internals were supplied by the Independent Magic Battalion in a joint effort by Sanada and Fujibayashi. It was capable of decoding nearly any coded radio transmission broadcast in the country.

"If Brother says so, then... Yuuka, you have my apologies for doubting you. I am sorry."

"It's fine. I was just thinking that this all does look pretty suspicious." She was talking about the timing of her showing up immediately after the attackers had been dealt with—or at least, that was Tatsuya's guess.

"But why would the police only set up a checkpoint on the road leading to the main house?" asked Miyuki.

Yuuka's smirk deepened, but then her expression turned serious as she met her passenger's gaze in the rearview mirror. "That, Miyuki, is because they don't want to let you in."

Yuuka's destination for the trio was a Tsukuba vacation house at the foot of Mount Amigasa in the Yatsugatake Mountains.

She led them into the living room, then sat herself down in a recliner—in place of a sofa, the room had six recliners with footrests—then began to outline her plan for what would come next. "We'll stay here tonight."

Miyuki shot Tatsuya a wordlessly questioning gaze, but before he could answer, Yuuka continued, "Tomorrow, we'll all go to the main house together, shall we? If we do that, nobody will be able to sneak a look at your driver's schedule."

Tatsuya nodded at his sister. Yuuka's question had been directed at her, after all, and Tatsuya figured that, one succession candidate to another, Miyuki should be the one to answer that question.

"We're very grateful for the offer."

"It's decided, then!"

"Wait just a moment," Miyuki said, bringing the smiling host up short.

Just then, the vacation home's housekeeper brought in drinks—black tea and sundries for all. And not a pot, either—cups were lined up on the table and filled two-thirds full with tea. Finally, the house-keeper set a milk pot and a sugar pot on the table, then left the living room.

"...For someone who's so fastidious about etiquette, she sure doesn't have much tact," murmured Yuuka, giving her three guests an apologetic look. "I'm sorry. Everyone in my family drinks black tea, so we didn't have any green tea or coffee on hand."

"Oh, not at all," said Miyuki with a pleasant smile, reaching for her cup.

"The table's a bit of a reach, isn't it? I'll put the side tables out." Yuuka made certain that Miyuki had pulled her hand back before touching a switch on the arm of her chair.

Side tables rose up from the right side of all four occupied recliners.

Minami had come around to Miyuki's right side, and giving Yuuka a smile, she reached for the milk pot and placed it, along with a saucer and cup of tea, on Miyuki's side table.

"Thank you," Miyuki said, picking up the cup and taking a sip. She cocked her head slightly, then poured just a bit of milk from the pot into her cup. Stirring it with her spoon, she then smiled at Minami pleasantly.

Minami put the milk pot back on the table, then returned to her own seat. In contrast to the curt service of the housekeeper, she had just displayed a maid's natural, careful attentiveness to her mistress.

"…My, how charming. Was that for my benefit?" said Yuuka to Minami with a smile in a not terribly successful bid to seem unruffled.

"Why no, not at all," said Minami in a completely neutral tone, her simple, polite bow hiding her expression.

She fully intended to rub Yuuka the wrong way, but with a slow exhale, Yuuka was able to avoid letting her irritation show. "Well…I suppose my housekeeper was the first to behave poorly, so perhaps we can call it even."

Tatsuya had watched the byplay silently, drinking his tea black. He set the cup down on its saucer before speaking up. "Now, to the matter at hand."

Yuuka recomposed herself in her chair, and Miyuki squared herself to face her directly. "We have several things we'd like to ask you."

"I don't suppose you're just going to demand I tell you what I'm really thinking." Yuuka's playful demeanor faded slightly, and her eyes shone with a keen edge.

Miyuki met her with a gaze as cold and clear as the winter sky. "That would be a meaningless thing to ask."

Yuuka had the sudden feeling that she might lose her soul in those eyes and broke her gaze—then immediately looked back. "It wouldn't be totally useless. So long as it's something I can discuss, I'll speak my true mind."

"Is that so? Well, in that case… How was it that you were able to come to our aid at such a precisely convenient moment?"

"That *would* seem suspicious, wouldn't it?" Yuuka muttered with a dull grin. "But I'm not involved in any secret collusion. I hope you can believe that much."

"Certainly. But I would like to know the reason why."

"…The truth is, I was following your car."

Miyuki looked to Tatsuya. Tatsuya shook his head faintly.

Yuuka noticed this and was about to ask what it meant, but Miyuki was first to speak.

"I see," Miyuki said. "Why would you go to such lengths to help us?" she continued, in a tone of voice that made it sound like she didn't believe a word of Yuuka's explanation.

"Well—"

"I know you said that I needed a bodyguard, but you can't seriously expect to convince us with that argument now."

Yuuka sighed. "That's true… Fine. I'll be honest."

"Please do."

Yuuka looked uncomfortable under Miyuki's steady gaze but also didn't seem inclined toward any further deception.

"Tatsuya probably already knows about this, but…"

With that preamble, Tatsuya could see what Yuuka was about to say. He hadn't particularly wanted Miyuki to have to hear it, but if he cut Yuuka off here, there would be no way to resolve the situation. And if Miyuki were to be named successor, she needed to understand the motivations of the branch families.

"At the New Year's celebration, Maya is going to name you, Miyuki, as the next leader of the clan. Some of the branch families are trying to interfere. They believe that if you can be prevented from attending the party, it will at least avoid your succession being announced there."

Miyuki's face evinced no shock. "So does this mean that they don't want me to be the family head?" she asked in a hard voice.

"I think only Uncle Shibata feels that way." Yuuka's answer was cruelly clear.

"I see… I take it he would prefer Katsushige?"

"I don't think so, no," Yuuka said, just as clearly, even though her answer was inconsistent with what she'd just said.

"I'm sorry, I don't think I follow what you're—"

Yuuka explained, "Uncle Shibata *would* prefer that Katsushige be named successor, but I'm sure he knows that if you're chosen, there's nothing he can do about it. And he knows perfectly well who the better magician is between you and Katsushige. He's an excellent magician by *ordinary* standards."

Yuuka couldn't help but laugh. Miyuki didn't join her, but her estimation of the man was the same.

"So there you have it. There's no one who truly opposes your ascension to family leadership."

"...What about you yourself, Yuuka?"

"Me?"

Miyuki was curious about why Yuuka was discussing the matter of the next family leader as though it had nothing to do with her. Yuuka was, after all, one of the four remaining candidates for the position.

"I also feel that you're well suited to the role, Miyuki," replied Yuuka nonchalantly—so perfectly nonchalantly, in fact, that it made her answer sound insincere. Still, she was being entirely honest. "Well, that's slightly imprecise language. Two years ago, the Tsukuba family decided to support designating you as the successor. The reason I've remained involved in the selection process is to preserve the Tsukuba family's voice in the process. And of course, in case the other branch families back Katsushige, to oppose them."

"Why would you go to such trouble?" Miyuki's question was understandable.

"About ninety percent of it is rather straightforward. We really do think you should become the next family head," Yuuka said, but then her expression clouded over, as though she didn't want to say what came next. "The other ten percent is...guilt over my mother, I suppose."

Miyuki's expression shifted. It was a vague answer, but for Miyuki, it was plenty. "Well, if you're trying to make amends, you needn't bother. I'm aware that it isn't what Touka wanted. But the reality is that she still personally followed the orders that my aunt gave, is it not?"

Touka was Yuuka's mother and the current head of the Tsukuba family. Yuuka's father wasn't dead—but Touka had already been the family head when they'd married, and he'd taken her name.

Touka specialized in mental interference magic, and she was known in the Yotsuba family as being an expert in a special kind of magic known as "Oath." The Oath was made with the consent of the target, and it placed semipermanent limits on their mental activity. It wasn't possible to unilaterally bind someone's mind—there had to be a key created that would release the target irrespective of the caster's will—but it was still an extremely powerful form of magic that made a sort of mind control possible, while still preserving the target's sense of self.

The magic was of particularly deep significance to Miyuki and Tatsuya. After their mother, Miya, had passed away, it had been Touka who cast Oath to seal away Tatsuya's magic abilities using Miyuki's power.

"There's nothing more I can say about that. I have no intention of hiding behind the excuse that it was done on the orders of the family head."

"…My apologies. I'm the one who asked about this, and then I let myself get worked up about it."

"It's understandable, from your perspective, Miyuki. I'm not offended."

"I believe I understand the position of the Tsukuba family now," said Miyuki in a bid to change the subject, eliciting a nod and a faint smile from Yuuka. "But why are members of the other branch families trying to postpone the announcement? If you happen to know, do please tell me."

Yuuka glanced at Tatsuya.

Tatsuya gave no response—not even to try to stop her.

Yuuka turned away from Miyuki's steady gaze and began to speak with downcast eyes. "Uncle Shibata and Uncle Mashiba want to separate you from Tatsuya, Miyuki. No, they want to separate Tatsuya from the heart of the Yotsuba clan and put him out to pasture somewhere, isolated from the world."

Miyuki took several deep breaths. They were ragged at first, but after five or six repetitions, she was able to compose herself. "...Not just society but the world as a whole?"

"Yes. Some of that is my conjecture, but I'm quite sure I'm right. I don't know why, but my uncles want to unmake Tatsuya, as a magician. They're interfering with the announcement that you will be the next clan leader in order to buy time for that."

"How does delaying my appointment have anything...anything at all...to do with trapping my brother?" Miyuki stuttered, trembling with rage.

"Miyuki, please—please try to calm yourself and listen to me. If you are named the heir, then as your Guardian, Tatsuya's position within the family would also be assured. He would become the elder brother of the next family head and her confidant. That's not something the heads of the branch families will be able to ignore."

Yuuka saw Miyuki's expression change. For the time being, she regained her composure.

"So they're trying to postpone your appointment until Minami there can step in as Tatsuya's replacement."

"...So that's how it is, is it?" Miyuki's voice was eerily cool and calm.

Yuuka had been trying her best not to be intimidated by Miyuki, but at this, she involuntarily shivered. "Y-yes. I'm very sure."

"On the other hand, if I do make it on time for New Year's, Brother's position will be assured." Miyuki, however, wasn't thinking about getting back at anybody or trying to hurt anybody else—nothing so dangerous or violent. The only thing on her mind was thwarting this unspeakable plot to separate her brother from her. "Yuuka, we cannot depart today, can we?"

Though none of them had eaten lunch, midday was well past. There was still a fair amount of daylight left, and if they were to set out right then and there, it was theoretically possible to reach the main house before it got too late.

"No...the police are still on the move. We haven't done anything illegal, but if we're detained by the police, it will cost us time. I think it would be best to wait until tomorrow."

"I understand. In that case, we shall take your advice. And thank you for your help today."

"I apologize for the accommodations not being ideal, but please relax as best you can."

"Thank you so much. We'll be counting on you again tomorrow."

Miyuki's tone was polite and restrained, but the force behind her words froze Yuuka's soul. Yuuka managed a smile and with some effort forced herself to nod.

Tatsuya, Miyuki, and Minami ended up taking an early dinner in place of the lunch they hadn't eaten (the food was merely acceptable) before they were each led to their own private room for the evening.

Tatsuya stood in front of his opened travel bag, trying to decide what to do about his clothes—or more precisely, his equipment—for tomorrow. He'd packed Trident, his custom Silver Horn CAD. The question was whether or not to use what he was most familiar with instead of the more easily concealed Silver Torus.

If he was anticipating magical combat, then the gun-type Trident would be the right choice, but if it came to hand-to-hand combat where magic would need to be suppressed, the Silver Torus bracelet would be the way to go.

Just as Tatsuya was about to close the flap on his bag, there was a knock at his door.

"Who is it?" he asked.

"It's Miyuki," came the reply.

Tatsuya left the bag open and turned to the door. "What's up?" he asked after he opened the door. She was alone.

"I just…wanted to talk a bit."

Maybe it was his imagination, but she looked a bit forlorn.

"Sure. Come on in." Tatsuya gestured for her to enter.

Miyuki first went over to where Tatsuya's bag was opened and then began folding and straightening his somewhat disarrayed clothing.

He was about to take a shower, after which he'd grab a fresh change of clothes, so there wasn't much point in repacking his bag at that moment, but Tatsuya didn't stop her. "You don't have to, but thanks" he said.

"Not at all; I enjoy doing it," she offered, a bit of happiness creeping into her voice. Seemingly satisfied, she closed the travel bag and turned to face its owner properly.

"You can sit on the bed, if you want," he suggested as he sat in a chair pulled out from the room's writing desk.

Miyuki dropped lightly on the bed without any noticeable reservations.

"So—you said you wanted to talk?"

At the prompt, Miyuki seemed to almost pout—her cheeks didn't literally puff, but a pout-like aura emanated from her nonetheless. "Do I have to have a reason to come see you?"

"No, of course not," he replied, immediately capitulating. He was unflappable whether he was facing crying children to angry police, but his sister's moods were another matter entirely.

Miyuki giggled. "I'm joking," she said, her mood immediately brightened by the agreeability. "And there *is* something I wanted to ask you."

So why didn't you just ask it in the first place? he wondered—but of course refrained from voicing the thought aloud. "What is it?" he eventually landed on.

"You knew about the branch houses' motives, didn't you, Brother?"

The question of how to throw her off the scent disappeared in the time it took Miyuki to blink.

"I did," he admitted. As Miyuki spent a moment deciding on her next question, he elaborated, "On the first day of the winter vacation, Mr. Kuroba visited me at FLT, which is when I found out. What he said was more or less the same as what Yuuka told us earlier. Yuuka said that some of it is her conjecture, but I think she has confirmation."

"Uncle Kuroba...? Then—"

Tatsuya, seeing what his sister was beginning to worry about, quickly interrupted to correct her. "The Kuroba family isn't involved with this interdiction operation. Mr. Kuroba told me himself that they were neutral, and I think we can believe him. And of course, neither Fumiya nor Ayako are our enemies."

"I see..." Miyuki sighed in relief, but she soon looked back up at Tatsuya with a serious gaze. "Why didn't you tell me about any of this?"

While he understood why she was upset at him about this, he had his own take on it. Tatsuya didn't look away from his sister. "The important thing is to prevent them from interfering. So long as you attend the gathering on New Year's as planned, it doesn't matter who's pulling the strings. I didn't want to make you worry more than you needed."

The current objective, from Tatsuya's perspective, was very simple. There was no need to discover where their enemy was hiding or when they might attack. The only thing that mattered was forcing their way past anyone who tried to stop them. Worrying about the details would simply put them at a disadvantage.

However, this was not a way of thinking that Miyuki could accept. "Maybe it doesn't help for me to think about any of that stuff, but it's still my right to be as worried about my brother as I please! Being able to cry over you or get angry on your behalf is very important to me. I don't consider any of that 'unnecessary'!" She promptly turned away, fuming.

Baffled by this outburst and eager to mollify her, Tatsuya stood and tried to place himself back within her line of sight. "Miyuki..."

He reached out to place his hand on her shoulder and caught nothing but air—not because she had brushed him off, but rather because Miyuki suddenly stood and embraced him.

"Brother, you do remember...?"

"Remember what?" he asked, but a memory was already vaguely coming back to him.

It was last year, the fourth day of the Nines, the first night of the rookies' battle. Miyuki had come to Tatsuya after he'd rejected having the Active Air Mine added to the index under his name, and...

"My feelings have not changed one bit since then. And they never will," Miyuki said, like she knew exactly what had just popped into his mind.

"I am on your side," she continued, as though she could see his memory with her own eyes.

"And I will always be on your side," she added, as though she were with him in the memory.

"The time will come. It will come. I know it will. I said it would." Miyuki looked up and met Tatsuya's gaze. Contrary to his expectations, she wore a beautiful smile.

"I believe that time is finally near. It might be a little bit different from what we pictured that night, but soon, Brother, you will be able to finally spread your wings and fly."

But hidden in the depths of that beautiful smile, Tatsuya could see a flicker of darkness. And that was what worried him more than anything else.

When Maya Yotsuba, current head of the Yotsuba family, received the report from her butler, Hayama, that Miyuki had been the target of two consecutive days of interference and was currently staying at the Tsukuba vacation house, she couldn't help but smile.

"What pointless games," she said, not with a sneer but a soft, murmured laugh.

The butler Hayama's appraisal was politely phrased and severe. "It would appear the branch families have underestimated Tatsuya's abilities."

"The village's bounded field wouldn't be able to withstand Tatsuya's dismantling, so if they're really in danger of not making it in time, they can still opt to fly in from above. And if it comes to that, it'll become a major incident. Anyone who can use Awareness Block magic won't get a lick of sleep until the bounded field is repaired, which itself won't be an easy task." Maya sighed fetchingly. "I wonder if they understand that if it comes to that, the responsibility will fall upon the branch houses who attempted to interfere with my orders?"

Maya sipped from her teacup, a frown furrowing her delicate brow.

"Aoki and that cohort notwithstanding, all of the branch family heads should have received accurate information."

"They have, ma'am." Hayama answered the implied question, then carefully refilled his mistress's cup with noncaffeinated herbal tea.

Within the Yotsuba family, Hayama, Hanabishi, Aoki, and Obara were all formally referred to as *butlers*, but in fact the word referred to eight people who supervised various servants within each section, and the only one who dealt solely with internal household business in a way that actually matched up with the term *butler* was Hayama.

It was evening, the time for a quiet, private cup of tea, which was why Maya spoke her mind so freely. She would never have done so in front of others. But the truth was the contempt she held for the whole pack of branch families—and indeed, the Yotsuba clan as a whole—was Maya's true self.

Hayama took all this in dispassionately, and finally, respectfully, offered his own view, thereby avoiding being entangled in his mistress's irritation. "Be that as it may, these delaying tactics might not be entirely pointless. Per Hanabishi's report, we have succeeded in significantly weakening the Anti–Great Asian Alliance hard-liners, the Great Asian Alliance reconciliation faction, and those who stand in opposition to the ten families. In particular, the artificial psychics stationed at Matsumoto Base were almost entirely wiped out. I very much doubt that their ilk will darken our doorstep ever again."

"I was never worried about artificial psychics," said Maya with a casual chuckle, her voice devoid of the venom it had had earlier. "In any case, this should wrap up our end-of-year housecleaning, yes?"

Hayama allowed himself a faint smile. "The arrangements have changed slightly, but Hanabishi informs me that, if anything, this means fewer people will be necessary."

"I daresay it does. After all the effort spent luring them out, Tatsuya handled all the fisticuffs entirely on his own." Maya made a faintly exasperated expression. "But no matter. Have you seen to the preparations for the New Year, Hayama?"

"Indeed, ma'am. Now all we need do is wait for Ms. Miyuki's arrival."

"Well, we've nothing to worry about, then."

"Ma'am, do you really not wish to stop Shibata?" the butler asked after a moment of hesitation. Hayama was aware of the Shibata family head's plan to have Katsushige Shibata and his Guardian stop Miyuki from reaching her destination. Naturally, Maya also knew.

Maya, for some reason, smiled a satisfied smile. "Not even Katsushige can stop Tatsuya."

While Katsushige Shibata was clearly among the finest combat magicians in the Yotsuba family, Maya estimated the chances of his delaying anything to be roughly zero.

In that moment, she saw in her mind a vision of Tatsuya taking the young man down.

[5]

The morning of December 31, Tatsuya, Miyuki, and Minami departed the Tsukuba villa in the hopes that the third time would be the charm.

Normally it would take two hours to drive from the villa to the Yotsuba headquarters. If they had to slow down owing to snowy conditions en route, that figure could rise to three hours. Yuuka had suggested that they needn't leave until after lunch, but Tatsuya was anticipating further interference and therefore decided to leave as early as was possible.

Being a night owl, Yuuka was visibly sluggish behind the wheel, as though her body hadn't fully awakened, which was probably why she'd suggested a later departure.

Nonetheless, her driving of the sedan was entirely safe, and soon they approached the tunnel that would lead to the small settlement controlled by the Yotsuba.

The tunnel diverged in the middle, and the branch that led to the village used an automatic gate with typeless magic as its key, only opening after receiving a particular pattern of psionic waves. This isolated the Yotsuba headquarters from the outside world—at least to surface traffic.

This arrangement was originally meant to conceal Lab Four, whose existence was a carefully guarded secret. Even those government and military officials who knew its name weren't told its location. When the Yotsuba family had inherited the facility, they literally erased the knowledge of its existence from the memories of those who'd known, thus ensuring the perfect secrecy of their headquarters' location.

There were a few other similar gates, but this was the only one that operated twenty-four hours a day, which made it the obvious place for an ambush. However, it was also subject to constant surveillance by the Yotsuba family, so anyone planning such a thing would have to be very well prepared.

For this reason, Yuuka had argued that they wouldn't be attacked here.

Tatsuya, however, was certain that they would be.

This explained the difference in their reactions to what happened next.

There on the mountain road, just before they entered the tunnel—a tsunami of white came crashing down the slope toward them.

"Miyuki, melt the avalanche!" Tatsuya commanded, a split second before Yuuka noticed the approaching wall herself.

"I'm on it!" the girl answered.

Yuuka slammed on the brakes.

"Minami, hemispherical shield, now!"

"O-okay!"

The avalanche thundered down toward the road from both sides.

Miyuki's magic turned the snow to water.

The car stopped.

A dome-shaped barrier encircled the car.

All of this happened in less than a second.

A muddy flood of water flowed around the car.

The avalanche had never been meant to directly impact the vehicle.

As the water from the liquefied avalanche drained away, Tatsuya ordered Minami to dispel her magic: "Minami, take down the shield."

"Understood." She unwove her spell before it could naturally dissipate.

Both Tatsuya's and Minami's faces were tense. Tatsuya got out of the car and stood in front of it. Minami, Miyuki, and Yuuka followed, a step behind him.

Boulders and felled trees blocked the road ahead of them, carried there by the avalanche-turned-flood. The four walked right up to the rubble.

"Brother, was stopping us here the point of this?" Miyuki asked, having realized the avalanche had not been aimed to hit them directly.

Tatsuya, however, had come to a slightly different conclusion. "No, this is an ambush."

"Show yourselves!" Yuuka shouted. "Otherwise, I won't hold back!" Her pride seemed to have been wounded by the fact that a car she was driving had been attacked here, at the very threshold of the Yotsuba house.

Furious at the lack of response, Yuuka produced a folding CAD from her handbag, pressed a button on its side, and opened it to reveal a numerical keypad.

Folding CADs had been introduced in the current year, with the lid of the opened section functioning as an aim-assistance antenna. Where a gun-type CAD was pointed at the target, with a folding CAD, the flat side of the antenna panel faced the target.

It was a new product from FLT, incorporating the general-purpose CAD and aim-assistance system developed in Düsseldorf two years earlier, but it had come not out of Tatsuya's Section 3 lab but rather from the company's main development team. Tatsuya had largely perfected the technology at the Nines the year before, but he'd only proposed incorporating the know-how that came from integrating assisted-aim systems into general-purpose CAD OSs. They honestly had yet to show a performance advantage over regular general-purpose CADs and were unlikely to appeal to anybody except early-adopter hobbyists—apparently Yuuka was something of an enthusiast.

However, regardless of the CAD used as a medium, the mental interference magic Yuuka cast was no joke.

"Mandrake" was an emanation of psionic energy radiating outward in a 150-degree arc that caused psychological damage to its targets in the form of pure terror.

Mandrake didn't create terrifying images but rather terror itself. Rather than destabilize a target's consciousness to let innate emotions run wild, it simply created the experience of terror.

The effects were not lethal, but those caught in its area of effect would experience extreme dread regardless of their psychological resilience, undermining their mental state considerably. In fact, the effects could be worse on those who'd been trained to resist fear. Assailed by an emotional response they had supposedly overcome, they tended to panic. Targets would either become catatonic or, unable to bear the strain, lose consciousness. Depending on the person, the lingering psychological damage could be significant.

There was another technique with similar effects called "Phobos," but while Phobos used psionic light as its medium, Mandrake used psionic waves—in other words, the "sound" of psions.

Because Mandrake was carried not via literal sound waves but by psionic "sound," acoustic isolation provided no defense against it. However, if isolation was achieved by magical means, that was a different story. The sound-deadening effect could travel though the psionic field, attenuating it.

As it was right now.

Just as Yuuka had cast Mandrake, immediately across from her, another spell had been cast—the acoustic attenuation magic of "Silent Veil."

Silent Veil couldn't entirely negate Mandrake, but it could lower its effectiveness—and when the spell was weakened, even a magician with no aptitude for mental interference magic could defend against it by boosting their own psionic fields.

But in order to use this technique, it was crucial to know in advance that the opposition was going to use Mandrake. And there was only one person who was both familiar with Yuuka's background and specialties and could cast Silent Veil.

"This magic… Kotona, right? I know it's you. Show yourself! And Katsushige—stop hiding behind a woman and face us!"

Immediately following Yuuka's provocations, a shimmering heat mirage appeared directly in front of her. This wasn't just because of the moisture that lingered on the asphalt evaporating, but also because of the introduction of a layer of hot air above the rapidly heating asphalt itself.

"Ah, Phonon Maser." Tatsuya spoke the name of the spell out loud, to help calm Miyuki and Minami, who were still rattled from the rapid sequence of events.

"I am not hiding," said a clear, low voice in front of them.

Yuuka looked up, shielding her eyes from the sun with her hand. Miyuki and Minami did likewise. Only Tatsuya kept his eyes on the boulder that had fallen in the middle of the road. Emerging from the shadow it cast came three people: two men and a woman.

"It merely took some time to get around this obstacle."

The man was a head taller than Tatsuya, with a slim build, at over six feet tall. He looked skinny, which kept him from appearing slow-moving the way men of greater stature often did—it didn't seem like the world's number-one heavyweight boxer would have particularly intimidated him. This man was in his first year as an official in the Ministry of Defense, the scion of the Shibata family, and a candidate for the next leader of the Yotsuba family: Katsushige Shibata.

"If you weren't hiding, why didn't you answer me immediately?" sneered Yuuka.

"I planned to address you from a more reasonable distance," he called, sticking out a hand to hold back the indignant young man who stood next to him. "You are the one who shot before asking any questions. You're as belligerent as you ever were, Yuuka." He punctuated his statement with a sad shake of his head.

Yuuka's eyes narrowed viciously at his condescension. "You're really going to say that after hiding in the shadows and sucker punching us with an avalanche? Okay..."

"It was set on a path that would avoid collision with your car. There was no malicious intent."

"That's right!" said the young man Katsushige had held back, unable to restrain himself any longer. "And I made sure that Phonon Maser didn't hit you, either! Unlike the way *you* came at *us*."

Evidently the Phonon Maser had been his doing.

"Kanata, would you please restrain yourself?" Yuuka said with deliberate contempt in her voice, snapping at the bohemian-looking young man. His dress and affect made him look like a musician or artist of some kind.

"What—?"

"I'm talking to Katsushige right now. The heiress to the Tsukuba family is talking to the heir to the Shibata family. This is no time for servants to be butting in."

"Why, you—!"

"Kanata, stop."

It was a woman standing on the other side of Katsushige who spoke up to restrain Kanata—a woman named Kotona.

"But, Sis—"

The young man's full name was Kanata Tsutsumi, and he, along with his older sister, served the Shibata family by acting as Katsushige's Guardians.

"It is simply fact that we are Katsushige's servants. Nothing in what Yuuka just said is incorrect."

"But c'mon—"

"Don't embarrass Katsushige."

At this, Kanata stepped back.

"Aww, Katsushige, your underlings really like you," Yuuka spat, her voice dripping with sarcasm. "It's not just Kotona who *adores* you, hmm?" she continued pointedly, causing Kanata's face to redden.

But Katsushige's unperturbed bass voice forestalled the man's explosion. "Indeed, thank you. They're wasted on me, I must confess. I am constantly striving to be a master of them, but I feel that to truly follow the ways of the Yotsuba, I should be less emotional. I have much to learn from you in that respect, Yuuka."

This time it was Yuuka whose face flushed red.

"I'm merely a Guardian myself, but if I might be permitted a word," interjected Tatsuya just in time to save Yuuka from a disgraceful display.

"Certainly. Guardian or not, you are a close blood relative of the family head. I don't consider you to be of notably different status when speaking to Yuuka or me, Tatsuya."

It was difficult to tell whether Katsushige's easy demeanor was the familiarity of a man chatting with a younger relative, or the unconcerned ease of a man addressing himself to his servant. In point of fact, Miyuki herself wasn't exactly sure how to address or treat Katsushige, but of course Tatsuya wasn't concerned about such matters.

"Thank you. I will make this quick," Tatsuya said, completely unruffled by it all.

"Oh? Do tell."

"It's a simple request." True to his word, Tatsuya came right to the point: "Let us pass."

"I see. That's the sort of directness I've come to expect from you."

"You'll have to excuse me," Tatsuya said politely—but he neither bowed nor took his eyes off Katsushige. He merely waited for the answer.

The man met Tatsuya's directness with his own. "Unfortunately, I can't let you pass." His eyes glittered with intimidation. "Allow me to make my request as well—turn away from this path and go back the way you came. If you do, there will be no more need for fighting."

Tatsuya nodded wordlessly, but not because he was acceding to Katsushige's demand. It was a gesture of comprehension. "So you're saying that a fight is unavoidable if we wish to pass here."

Katsushige pressed his lips together. To his right and left, Kotona and Kanata became visibly nervous. "That's correct."

Katsushige had meant his statement to conclude the affair—but Tatsuya continued. "In that case, I have a proposal."

Internally, Katsushige had prepared a magic program and only needed to fire it—but he released the effort required to hold it and let it disperse. "...I'm listening."

Kotona and Kanata held their CADs at the ready. Across from them, Minami appeared similarly ready to throw up a barrier at the slightest provocation.

And then Tatsuya faced Katsushige and said something completely unexpected. "This probably goes without saying, but the Guardians of Yotsuba family are magicians who protect their master or mistress from any danger."

"And?"

"As Miyuki's Guardian, I do not particularly wish to put her in the middle of a dangerous battlefield. I'm sure the same is true for your two Guardians."

"Of course it is!" Kotona hissed. "I don't want this family dispute to put Katsushige in any danger!" The tone in her voice laid bare her feelings; she was protecting someone she loved.

"I feel the same way as my sister," Kanata noted.

Tatsuya nodded solemnly.

"Wait, don't tell me—" Katsushige started, seeming to suddenly suspect that he was about to be caught in a trap.

"We want to pass. You don't want to let us," Tatsuya said, cutting Katsushige off. "To break this standoff, combat is inevitable. In which case—"

"Wait!"

"Let a battle between the Guardians decide it. I'm alone. I'm willing to face both of yours."

"No!"

"Fine with me."

Katsushige and Kotona gave opposing answers simultaneously.

Tatsuya ignored it and concluded his thought: "As we have a neutral third party here, Yuuka, I'll have Minami protect both her and Miyuki. You have my word—I won't let them interfere."

"Please let me fight!"

"No, it's too dangerous!" Katsushige argued with his Guardians, not even waiting to hear the end of Tatsuya's statement. "Tatsuya isn't the defective magician everybody thinks he is. I'm not even certain that I could defeat him myself. The previous Yotsuba family head, Eisaku, dedicated his life to raising Tatsuya as a combat magician from the moment he was born!"

"We're second-generation Bard series engineered magicians, made for combat! We can fight, too! Combat was written into our genes from *before* we were even born. I don't care who our opponent is; they won't beat us that easily!"

"That's not the issue! Compared to you, Tatsuya might as well be in another dimension! He first killed someone when he was six years old, immediately after the conclusion of the artificial magician experiments. It wasn't an accident or a misfire—seconds after gaining his newfound power, he slaughtered a seasoned thirty-year-old combat magician without hesitation. He was just six years old! He wasn't even out of elementary school!"

Kotona's eyes went wide.

She wasn't the only one at a loss for words. Minami and even Miyuki also looked stricken.

"Kotona, what were *you* doing when you were six?"

She couldn't answer his question.

"Katsushige," Tatsuya warned, the only one willing to take up the silence. "Please don't casually talk about other people's private lives like that."

He met Tatsuya's gaze, then looked to Miyuki and Minami, his expression turning sickeningly awkward.

"Master, please let us do this," Kanata said, breaking in to reinforce his sister's plea. He said *master* like he was addressing the proprietor of a coffee shop. "It's true that he looks like he'll be tough. Just looking at him, I can feel the hair on the back of my neck standing up. But with both of us, I'm sure we can take him."

Katsushige scowled. "That's what he's counting on you to think."

"Then let him think that! It'll give us the advantage."

"Still..."

As Katsushige searched for a sufficiently convincing counterargument, Miyuki spoke up. "Katsushige Shibata," she said, intoning his full name in a soft, polite, and terrifyingly cold tone.

Standing beside Tatsuya, she looked straight at Katsushige with a clear, sharp gaze. "My aunt, the head of the Yotsuba family, has ordered my presence at the New Year's celebration to be held on New Year's Day. In order to comply with this order, I must arrive at the main house today."

Miyuki's beautiful intonation and perfect diction made her words sound almost musical, and they left no room for any interruption, much less a rebuttal.

"Interfering with my arrival is the same as interfering with my aunt's orders. Your words and actions are tantamount to revolt against the head of this family. The Shibata family will be declaring open rebellion against the Yotsuba family. Of course you understand the implication of this, do you not?"

Katsushige was stuck for an answer. He'd come fully prepared to be labeled a traitor, but he wasn't so stubborn as to just agree with the proposition that the Shibata family was openly defying the Yotsubas.

Miyuki smiled angelically. It wasn't the smile of one neighbor to another but rather the smile a judge might give a sinner. "But you have your own position. So rather than report your actions to my aunt, I am willing to let my brother decide this. If my brother loses, I will withdraw as you've asked me to."

It wasn't a proposal; it was a threat. Katsushige had been prepared to accept being labeled a traitor, but now somehow the entire Shibata family had been taken hostage, and he was cornered.

"Unfortunately, I cannot give you much time to decide. Please tell me your decision."

"...I will fight Tatsuya. Or may I not?" Katsushige demanded bitterly.

Miyuki inclined her head apologetically. "I said I would defer to my brother. And you have already heard his thoughts."

Katsushige continued to agonize, unaware that he was caught in a mental trap laid by Tatsuya.

Ordinarily, there would have been no cause for him to worry so. He'd come here with the specific purpose of using force to compel the Shiba siblings to turn around. That had been his intention all along, so he didn't need Miyuki's permission to fight the guy.

Of course, his half-baked plan was really just another reason he was trapped. He didn't have to negotiate with them to know that neither Miyuki nor Yuuka would just obediently pull a U-turn at his request. Force was going to be required eventually—he didn't need a final consultation with Kotona and Kanata to know that the three of them would unquestionably attack.

And thanks to his misbegotten hope that the situation could be resolved with words, what ought to have been an all-versus-all face-off had been turned into a battle with conditions attached. Instead of being able to help absorb some of their opponents' power, Katsushige had been forced to expose Kotona to danger. And when he should have been able to say "I refuse," he'd now been denied that option.

He outplayed badly enough that time was now conspicuously passing as he tried to find a way out—until finally, Kotona came to her master's rescue.

"I, Kotona Tsutsumi, accept this challenge in the place of my master, Katsushige Shibata!"

"Kotona!" shouted Katsushige as he tried to forestall her, but this time she would not be held back.

"Katsushige, there is no other way. To avoid open conflict within the family, you specifically chose not to engage in a preemptive ambush attack, so this is a preferable outcome for you. No matter the result, no succession candidates will be injured or lost."

"That doesn't mean it's okay for me to lose *you*!"

"I won't be beaten so easily. I *will* win this fight. You'll see."

"But…Kotona, please…"

Kotona held her finger up to Katsushige's mouth, silencing the helplessly worried man.

"Katsushige, look at Miyuki," she said. "She believes in her brother absolutely. That is why she's unshaken."

Just as Kotona said, when Katsushige looked at Miyuki, she betrayed not a hint of concern.

"Won't you believe in me, too, Katsushige?" said Kotona in a sulky tone, a mischievous twinkle in her eye—but Katsushige knew that it was merely an act: Kotona's best effort to appear more confident than she felt.

Kotona understood Katsushige's fear. In the four days prior to their rendezvous with Kanata, she and Katsushige had discussed the danger posed by Tatsuya's dismantling and regeneration abilities. He knew that she had to be aware of his preternatural ability in combat.

His training had not been focused on providing protection but rather the singular pursuit of defeating his opponent. There was no time for Katsushige to explain quickly how despite being a magician, Tatsuya had also been trained in silencing his enemies with a variety of weapons. The one example he'd been able to give ought to suffice for Kotona to understand the danger she faced.

And still she put on a brave face and asked him to believe in her. It left him no choice.

"…All right. I'll trust you two. Kotona, Kanata—win this."

"We got this!"

"We certainly do!"

The Tsutsumi siblings shouted their assent, then stepped forward to face Tatsuya.

With a wave, Tatsuya gestured for Miyuki to stand back.

Katsushige likewise retreated. As he did so, he used magic to push the boulders and felled trees clear from the road, the better to see Kotona and Kanata's fight through to its end.

Tatsuya turned to face the sibling Guardians again, a strangely apologetic look on his face. "Sorry to pour cold water on this heartfelt exchange, but I have no intention of killing either of you."

Kotona reddened. "I-if you think saying that's gonna make us go easy on you, think again!"

"That wasn't a ruse."

"Well, fine then! We're still not gonna let up on you!" Kanata shouted past gritted teeth, trying to cover up his embarrassment.

From Tatsuya's perspective, his opponents were misunderstanding him and willfully taking offense, but if he pointed that out, the terms they'd finally managed to settle on would probably go right out the window. In any case, Tatsuya thought, he and his sister had been delayed two days. If anyone threatened to delay them further, he didn't think he'd be able to *hold himself back.*

"So shall we start here? Or would you prefer a different location?"

Kotona glanced over her shoulder. She'd meant only to check that there was sufficient distance between her and Katsushige, but when she caught his eye, he silently nodded, and she felt impatient and excited despite herself. "Here is fine."

"Well, then."

Just as Tatsuya spoke the words, Kotona's body flew into the air.

"Kotona!"

Ahead of her, Kanata attacked Tatsuya. But Katsushige didn't follow him long enough to see the outcome. His attention was on Kotona, who'd been flung into the air with a flight effect that seemed to be a variation of gravity-control magic.

Katsushige reached out to try to come to Kotona's aid—the shock of having been thrown so suddenly skyward made it impossible for her to slow her fall or assume a better landing posture.

Inertial control magic to neutralize the g-forces on her body.

Deceleration magic to slow her fall to the ground.

Kinetic magic to adjust the arc of her fall toward him.

Using his portable terminal-style CAD, Katsushige keyed three magic programs in rapid succession and directed them at Kotona.

Rather than casting the magic as a single program with three steps, he used three discrete spells, his rapid, careful sequencing avoiding interference and ensuring that she landed precisely where he intended her to—in his arms.

"Th…thank you," she said, shamefaced even as he cradled her.

Katsushige hid his profound relief as he set her down.

"My apologies. I was so fixated on the dismantling attack I was expecting that…I left myself wide open to other magic."

"Watch yourself. Tatsuya can flash cast things besides Dismantle and Regenerate, now. I've explained this several times already."

"Yes, sir…"

"His flash-cast strength is only third-rate, but his activation speed is the quickest in all of the Yotsuba. His ability to repeatedly cast the same magic in an instant makes up for what he lacks in strength. You experienced it just now, right?"

"Yes."

"As long as you understand. Go. Your brother is struggling."

"Understood."

Having warned Kotona as best he could, Katsushige sent her back out, suppressing the urge he felt to go in her place.

Taking advantage of the gap in Kanata's attention that seeing his sister flung into the air opened, Tatsuya reached out and placed his palm on Kanata's chest, right over his heart, firing a virtual wave oscillation into it.

But before the wave could reach Kanata's heart, it was canceled out by another wave that flowed through Kanata's body. Tatsuya's magic was overwritten by the interference.

Kanata rolled backward, then snapped the fingers of his left hand.

Before the snap could become a thundering crash washing over him, Tatsuya dismantled the sound-amplification effect powering it. But as he did so, he let Kanata pull back out of range.

"Trying to sucker punch me, huh? Fine by me!" Kanata waved his pistol-shaped CAD in an arc, pulling the trigger repeatedly.

Each trigger pull caused a sound-emitting magic program to appear in midair. It was Acoustic Cannon, which blasted sound waves at energy levels that could temporarily interfere with the human body's functioning.

Tatsuya dismantled each one in turn, rendering them powerless.

"Damn, so that's 'Program Dispersion,' huh?" Apparently Kanata was the kind of person who narrated whatever was happening. Maybe it was his way of encouraging himself—the effect on his morale was undeniable. But as far as Tatsuya was concerned, it was both a waste of effort and a vulnerability.

Tatsuya filled his body with psions, using them—rather than mere nerves—to control his physical movements.

"Fine, how about this?" shouted Kanata, leveling his CAD at Tatsuya.

But by the time he did, Tatsuya was already upon him.

This was *shukuchi*—not the mystical teleportation of fictional martial artists, but a true hand-to-hand combat technique.

It was one of the physical body control techniques Tatsuya had learned from Yakumo. He'd heard the term *shukuchi* from his teacher but didn't know if that was really its name. In any case, historically accurate naming conventions were not something Tatsuya was concerned about.

What mattered to him was its effect.

Kanata's eyes went wide as Tatsuya suddenly appeared right in front of him, *without having used acceleration-type magic.*

Before Kanata could react, Tatsuya slapped his CAD out of his hand, then landed a hard punch to his solar plexus.

Kanata folded with a grunt, collapsing to the ground.

The strike hadn't involved any vibration magic. It was pure martial arts, which meant that the vibrations Kanata had set up within his own body were completely useless as a defense.

Tatsuya had struck with the intent to render Kanata instantly unconscious. He wouldn't kill him, but short of that, he was unconcerned about any physical complications Kanata might suffer. But the soccer kick he aimed at Kanata's head was cut short.

Tatsuya leaped back, rendering the sonic explosions suddenly going off around him inert.

Katsushige sent Kotona back out immediately after Kanata's Acoustic Cannon shots were nullified. There had been thirty meters, at best, between Kotona and Kanata.

And yet, by the time she had closed to within ten meters, her brother was on the ground.

Kotona couldn't even take the time to call out his name before she activated her CAD.

The Bard series of engineered magicians were combat focused, specializing in vibration-type magic—particularly sonic interference. However, the term *combat focused* covered a wide variety of applications, and Kotona's skills were more focused on support—battle awareness, deception and camouflage, and damage reduction—than attack.

Her strongest abilities were Passive Sonar, Silent Veil, and Sonic Bomb. While technically an attack, Sonic Bomb was really a support technique better suited to restricting an enemy's movement rather than inflicting damage; its capacity to do so paled in comparison to her brother's Acoustic Cannon and Phonon Maser.

But with him in danger, she deployed her own attack magic as far and as densely as she could manage.

Sonic Bomb emanated acoustic energy in a spherical area from the point of its activation, and at this distance it normally would have hit both herself and her target. But both Kotona and Kanata constantly maintained a layer of sound information amplification between their bodies and the air immediately surrounding them. For the two of them, it was as natural as the Eidos Skin—the information amplification magicians used to protect their bodies from outside magic. Any physically harmful sound would be rendered harmless by it.

This had been the basis of her calculation when she'd unleashed as much attack magic as she could possibly muster.

But before Kotona's Sonic Bombs could become physical sound, each of them had been dismantled by Tatsuya's Program Dispersion.

"He targeted twenty-four separate locations at once?!" she shouted in dismay.

A bystander might suggest that she should have been readying her next move rather than pointing out the obvious, but that was easier said than done. She was shocked to her core at Tatsuya's capacity for nullifying magic, and it didn't occur to her that even this moment's hesitation would lead to an opening that Tatsuya could exploit.

Her opponent suddenly vanished from view.

He had merely jumped diagonally upward, but Kotona's eyes weren't quick enough to follow.

It was a simple leap with a moment's worth of acceleration magic applied to it. Since he hadn't used any inertial damping, the g-forces Tatsuya experienced were considerable, but he was used to them. And, crucially, because he'd used magic only momentarily, with no continuous effect, Kotona could neither track him with her naked eye nor with any magical senses.

He used another burst of acceleration magic in midair to change direction.

By the time Kotona's magic sense let her turn to face him, he was already too close for her to do anything else.

If he'd been attacking Kanata, Tatsuya would've kicked him into the air. But with Kotona, he was reluctant—not because he had suddenly developed a sense of chivalry but rather because an impact on Kotona's delicate body at this velocity might well have killed her.

As he hit the ground, Tatsuya reached for his opponent's neck and, using the remaining kinetic energy, pressed down.

Kotona's body *fell*, and careful not to injure her, Tatsuya caught her and lowered her to the ground.

As he recovered from Tatsuya's jab and came to, the first thing Kanata saw was his sister being held to the ground with Tatsuya's *hand around her throat*.

"Get away from her!" Kanata quickly snatched up the CAD he'd dropped, took aim at Tatsuya, and fired Phonon Maser.

If it hit him, even Tatsuya wouldn't escape unscathed. A highly skilled magician like Katsuto or Minami might have been able to erect a barrier that would have deflected it, but without a barrier in place, it would have been a fatal attack for anyone except Tatsuya.

But the Phonon Maser's beam simply stopped.

The instant after it was activated, its program was dismantled, and with the dissipation of the coherent waves that powered it, it seemed to vanish in midair.

Technically, the beam had hit Tatsuya. But the amount of time he was exposed to it was so short that it didn't even singe his clothing.

Shocked that his specialty had betrayed him, Kanata tried to activate it a second time. And a third and a fourth. "Why—?"

But each time, it was dispelled by Tatsuya and refused to re-cohere.

And then his opponent leaped again—toward him.

But this time, the attacker was struck in midair by an explosion of compressed air.

"Tatsuya!"

After hitting the ground, Tatsuya scrabbled to his feet at the sound of his sister's voice.

Miyuki allowed herself the briefest moment of relief before whirling on her heel. "Katsushige, what is the meaning of this?"

The blast had come from him. He did not answer Miyuki's question—but he did loose another blast.

This magic was Katsushige Shibata's specialty, and he was a candidate to become the next head of the Yotsuba family. His casting was so fast that Tatsuya's nullification couldn't keep up with it.

Katsushige specialized in density manipulation. It was a fundamental skill of convergence-type magic, and being so basic, it had a wide variety of applications. It was the manipulation and control of solid, liquid, and gaseous substances.

For example, selectively lowering the density of a volume within a solid substance could create a hole. The avalanche from earlier had been created by altering the distribution density of the snow on the mountain, sequentially creating spots on the slope where the snow was thinner.

By altering the density of a liquid, a high-pressure stream of that liquid could be created. It was also possible to direct a flow of liquid upstream, against the pull of gravity.

And by manipulating the density of a gas, he could make vacuum-like suction forces or explosive blasts of gale-force wind.

Unusually for a magician of the Yotsuba family, Katsushige had specialized in *normal* magic. But in his application of it to a huge variety of circumstances, the speed at which he cast it, the amount of simultaneous programs he could deploy, and the breadth of physical phenomena to which he could effect change, he was an excellent magician by any *normal definition*.

Seeing that his cancellation ability couldn't keep up with Katsushige's casting, Tatsuya instead directed his dismantling magic to the construct that was causing the variation in the air density.

The influence trying to create a high-pressure area—

—and the influence trying to dismantle the construct creating the air density differential—

—clashed with each other.

As a result, Katsushige's magic misfired.

"Wha—?!" Kanata croaked in dismay.

But unlike the Tsutsumi siblings, Katsushige didn't hesitate after his magic was thwarted. He had fully joined the fight and was already preparing his next attack.

However, he was brought up short by a sudden violent localized updraft. The gust wasn't enough to lift his body off the ground. In fact, the wind hadn't itself been created by magic.

The updraft focused around Katsushige was the result of magic that had been employed in the air above him.

The wind being sucked into the vortex overhead was being chilled by rapid depressurization, with the water vapor in the rarefied air condensing and freezing into tiny grains of ice.

The rapid depressurization itself was a byproduct of the fact that a large volume of nitrogen—which comprised almost 80 percent of the air—had been instantly liquefied.

With an influence far beyond anything Katsushige could match, Miyuki had cast Niflheim.

The mist of liquid nitrogen mixed with the vortex's swirling flow, then under the influence of gravity, began to fall as droplets of rain.

Above Katsushige, sleet poured down. The solid portion of the sleet was crystallized water, but the droplets were liquid nitrogen, registering at -200° centigrade.

Katsushige threw up a double-layered shield—a material deflector and vacuum seal.

The extreme low temperature that resulted from the vaporization of liquid nitrogen could be life-threatening even without direct contact with the droplets. Katsushige was temporarily trapped within his own barrier, his movement completely halted.

Tatsuya took three leaps.

Kanata tried to draw a bead on Tatsuya with his handgun CAD but was unable to follow Tatsuya's three midair direction changes.

Unlike his sister, Kanata was shown no mercy when Tatsuya kicked him into the air.

As Tatsuya looked down at the fallen bodies on the road, Miyuki came running up to him.

"Brother, are you okay?!"

—No attack came from Katsushige.

"Are you hurt?!" Miyuki asked, worried about any injuries Tatsuya might have sustained from being shot down by Katsushige's initial compressed-air round.

"I'm fine. I haven't sustained any wounds that need to be *rolled back*." Tatsuya smiled faintly.

"Thank goodness…" Miyuki breathed a sigh of relief.

Minami arrived beside them and held out a hand towel to Tatsuya. "Here, Tatsuya, you can use this."

"Ah, thanks."

Miyuki's keen gaze then fell not on Minami nor the white hand towel, but rather upon Katsushige. "Katsushige, I will ask you again. What was the meaning of your intervention?"

Before Katsushige could answer, Yuuka arrived at Miyuki's side and shouted a condemnation. "Katsushige, what you did here was a contemptible ambush. Not only did you break the terms of Tatsuya's fight with Kotona and Kanata, but you also committed an outrageous sneak attack. Explain yourself!"

"Miyuki, Yuuka," Tatsuya interrupted, "would you mind saving this conversation for a later day?"

It was Katsushige, formerly silent, who asked the obvious question: "Why?"

"If you don't attend to those two, they'll suffer complications." Tatsuya's answer was exactly what Katsushige was most concerned about. "Given modern medicine and magical healing techniques, there shouldn't be any lasting health issues, but I do think you should get them medical attention as soon as possible."

Tatsuya didn't wait for Katsushige to answer before looking back over his shoulder to his own sister. "We should get moving, too."

She nodded wordlessly. Not only did Miyuki have no desire to quibble with her brother's words, she showed not even a trace of discontent.

Tatsuya wiped his face with the towel, then handed it back to Minami. Minami took it and briskly refolded it.

Tatsuya turned to Yuuka. "Yuuka, would you be willing to drive us?"

Unlike Miyuki, Yuuka's brows knit in frustration. "Tatsuya, are you okay just leaving it like this?" she asked, glancing in Katsushige's direction.

Katsushige was currently applying healing magic to his Guardians with a desperate expression on his face. Even though he was alternating between the two rather than attempting to treat them simultaneously, it was still a high-level procedure that even a trained medical magician would have found challenging. The fact that he wasn't letting his personal feelings interfere reflected well on his sense of responsibility as their superior.

But the sight did nothing to repair Yuuka's low estimation of him after his interference in the battle that had just concluded.

"Am I okay leaving it like this? That's an odd question. I have no reason to condemn him in the first place," Tatsuya replied.

"Huh?" Yuuka gawked, surprised. "I mean, he blindsided you, didn't he?"

"His assignment was to prevent Miyuki from going past this point. I expected the three of them to attack us all at once from the very beginning, honestly."

Yuuka looked stunned. "*That's* why you sent Kotona flying toward Katsushige in the beginning?"

Tatsuya didn't reply to that. "Meanwhile, my goal was to ensure

Miyuki's safe attendance at the New Year's party. Allowing time for preparation before the event, this doesn't mean we have the luxury of arriving any time today. I would like to reach the headquarters as quickly as possible."

"I see…so as long as Katsushige doesn't interfere further, you don't care what happens." Yuuka glanced in the man's direction again.

He seemed to have finished administering first aid to Kotona, who had regained consciousness but was not yet sitting up. In any case, she had merely been rendered unconscious and had sustained no external injuries, so Katsushige's primary concern was that not too much time passed before she awoke. He was now crouched down next to Kanata, seeing to him.

"All right. If you're satisfied, I'll let it go for now. Let's move on."

The four got in their car, and Yuuka drove them onward.

As they passed by Katsushige, still tending to his charges, he didn't even look up.

[6]

It was three o'clock in the afternoon by the time they arrived at the Yotsuba headquarters.

The servants who received them led Yuuka away to the guesthouse the Tsukuba family always used, while Minami had been directed to stay in the four-person room she'd lived in before moving to Tokyo. Here at headquarters, she would be treated not as a guest but as staff, and even now she had probably changed into a domestic maid uniform and was pitching in to help with the household preparations for the coming day.

Tatsuya and Miyuki, meanwhile, were led to guest quarters in the main house—two connected Japanese-style rooms. Unlike Minami, Tatsuya was being treated as Miyuki's elder brother; he got the sense that the household staff were treating him differently than they normally would, but he allowed himself to be led along rather than stopping somebody and demanding to know the reason for the change.

"Pardon the intrusion."

The room's wooden door slid open—it was Minami, wearing a long-sleeved black dress with a white apron tied over it. She looked exactly as she had when Tatsuya and Miyuki had first met her.

Minami knelt and bowed so completely that her forehead touched the room's tatami mats. "Tatsuya, sir. Miyuki, miss," she went on, addressing them with stiff formality—and putting Tatsuya's name first.

"Minami, don't you think it would be better not to address us that way here?"

Tatsuya of course wasn't suggesting that she talk to them the way she always did—but if someone else happened to overhear her addressing him first and foremost, and with equal rank as his sister, he was concerned that Minami could end up incurring the suspicion of the senior housekeeper.

"No, I am bringing a message from Mrs. Shirakawa."

Mrs. Shirakawa presided over all housekeeping staff at the Yotsuba main house—put simply, she was the *chief maid*. Her husband was the sixth-ranking butler for the Yotsuba clan, and he assisted Hayama, the head butler who presided over the entire family staff.

"Sir, miss—you are both asked to come to the inner dining room at seven o'clock. Her Ladyship will receive you there," Minami finished, her diction smooth and perfect. "That is the message."

In other words, the *sir/miss* wording and order of address were from Mrs. Shirakawa, and Minami was merely repeating them as stated.

Tatsuya and Miyuki shared a look. So far as either of them could remember, Mrs. Shirakawa had never used *sir* to address Tatsuya.

Something was definitely up here at the headquarters of the Yotsuba family. And it involved Tatsuya, somehow.

He had the impression that it wasn't necessarily a bad development for him and Miyuki as siblings, but he still felt a vague unease over it.

But Miyuki was worried about something else, and in this environment, Miyuki's instincts were more perceptive. "The inner dining room? And my aunt will be waiting? She really said that?"

"Yes."

"...I wonder if there's something she wants to talk to us about before the celebration." Tatsuya hurriedly tried to guess at Maya's motivation.

The inner dining room was used for Maya's personal dinners. It wasn't a private dining area where she ate alone but rather a place where she received particularly important guests or where she discussed especially sensitive topics over dinner.

Tatsuya knew that tomorrow's gathering would be to announce the successor to the rest of the family. He'd deduced as much the moment he'd seen the invitation—or rather, the summons—and there was the evidence he got from Mitsugu Kuroba to consider as well.

He had to assume that the reason Miyuki was being summoned to the inner dining room had to have something to do with tomorrow's event.

"Minami—Fumiya and Ayako have already arrived, right? Were Yuuka and Katsushige also invited to dinner?"

"Fumiya and Ayako have been here since yesterday, I believe. Regarding Yuuka and Katsushige, I do not know."

"Huh."

Evidently Maya's dinner plans were not widely known to the mansion's staff. Tatsuya concluded that only a limited number of them would be involved in serving the dinner.

"Brother, if she wants to talk to us ahead of time, perhaps it really is about tomorrow—?" Miyuki said, noticing that Tatsuya was trying to buy a few moments to think. It was less a question than a confirmation.

"Yes. I imagine she's assembling all of the candidates to discuss what will happen tomorrow. I don't think any of the candidates are the type to make a scene if they're not chosen, but maybe Aunt Maya feels that she needs to deliver some instructions as a formality."

"Yuuka said she would decline, but doesn't Katsushige want the position?"

He had personally accepted involvement in the plot against Miyuki. Could it be that by preventing her from being named heir, he hoped to plant the seed for his own ascension? Miyuki seemed to think so.

Tatsuya disagreed. "No, I don't think that's it. If he wanted the position for himself, he wouldn't have dirtied his hands the way he did." He suspected that Katsushige had only resorted to force because he'd already given up on the position.

"That said, we won't know how things will shake out until the time comes. Ah, and, Minami," Tatsuya said, realizing there was something he needed to make certain of. "Was I invited to this dinner as well?"

The message from Mrs. Shirakawa had specified that Tatsuya and Miyuki were to come to the inner dining room.

Tatsuya had never eaten with anyone other than his sister at this mansion. He had never been invited to any group meals.

"Yes. Both you and Miyuki have been asked to attend, sir."

"Understood."

Minami bowed deeply again. "If you have need, please use that bell. I will attend you immediately." She gestured to a small handbell on a low table. She then stood, her duties concluded.

But Tatsuya stopped her short. "Minami."

"Yes?" She knelt down on the tatami floor again, facing him.

Tatsuya's request was simple. "I'd like you to see if Kuroba is available. If he is, please tell him that I'd like to meet with him as soon as possible. Just the two of us."

"Very well, sir," Minami agreed, then finally made good her exit.

Miyuki watched her go, then looked curiously to her brother. "Tatsuya, what do you want to talk to Uncle Kuroba for?"

"It's nothing major. There's just something I want to ask him."

"Would that have something to do the obstruction we encountered trying to get here?"

"Most likely. That's one of the things I'm going to try to confirm."

There was hesitation in Miyuki's eyes, and she looked away. When she spoke again, she did so without meeting Tatsuya's gaze, and her voice was tinged with frustration. "Why do you want to see him alone?"

"I just get the feeling that I should."

Tatsuya didn't sound especially convinced, and there was uncertainty in his eyes, too.

"Might I not come with you...?"

"I worry that Kuroba won't tell the truth if you do."

"But he will if it's just you?"

"I don't mean to imply that he considers me trustworthy or anything of the sort. Rather, he detests me enough not to hold back any of the awful, scandalous things he might want to say."

Miyuki opened her mouth as though to reply but then stopped short and nodded with lips pursed.

For a moment the two were silent. It was Miyuki who broke first.

"...I understand. I'll leave the conversation with Uncle Kuroba to you. In exchange, I want you to tell me what he said, even if it's just the parts that you think are all right for me to hear."

"Understood. But only after the celebration tomorrow is over. I don't want to burden your heart any more than it already has been."

"...All right."

It was just then that Minami returned.

"Tatsuya, sir, if I may?"

"Sure, c'mon in."

"Yes, sir." Minami slid the sliding door open as she had before and sat down beside the pair. "Mr. Kuroba says that he is available to meet you now, in his guesthouse."

Tatsuya noticed the worried look Miyuki gave him and answered it with a reassuring nod. "Okay. I'll take him up on that."

"Very well. I'll lead you there." Minami stood.

Tatsuya followed suit, and as he trailed Minami out of the room, he looked over his shoulder one last time and smiled. "It'll be fine."

Mitsugu Kuroba was staying in one of the compound's in-law suites—the one that happened to be his mother's full-time residence. She was the elder sister of both the former Yotsuba family head, Eisaku, and the head before him, Genzou.

She was therefore Tatsuya's grandfather's sister, but Tatsuya had never interacted with her even once. Unsurprisingly, it was his first time inside this guesthouse.

Minami led him to the entrance of the house, then handed him off to its housekeeper, who led Tatsuya to a living room set up to receive company.

Tea-serving implements had already been set out. When the housekeeper held up the iron kettle to pour water from it, steam quickly started to rise. She filled a small teapot with hot water, then served Tatsuya. It was only medium-quality green tea, rather than fine matcha, but Tatsuya had no intention of making requests.

The housekeeper put the teapot away but left the iron kettle out, perhaps to let it heat and humidify the room a bit. The water in the induction kettle gave off a gentle waft of steam without actually boiling.

Tatsuya was about a third of the way through his cup of tea when Mitsugu Kuroba entered the room.

"Sorry to keep you waiting."

The housekeeper who entered ahead of him refreshed Tatsuya's tea and placed a cup in front of Mitsugu.

"Not at all. I haven't been waiting long," Tatsuya said.

Mitsugu nodded and brought his tea to his lips.

He seemed considerably calmer than he had when he'd visited FLT a few days earlier. Either that, or with Miyuki's arrival at the main house, he'd accepted defeat and was making a virtue of necessity.

"So I believe you wanted to speak with me. What about?"

Tatsuya made a show of deliberately widening his eyes. "I've come to collect on the promise you made."

"Promise? Was there a promise?"

"There was." Tatsuya paused and took stock of Mitsugu's demeanor. Evidently, he wasn't going to admit the facts of his own volition, so Tatsuya decided to do it for him. "Five days ago, when we spoke at FLT, you promised you would tell me your reasoning if we were able to arrive here by the deadline."

Mitsugu clicked his tongue in irritation. He seemed to be regretting his carelessness, but Tatsuya was not going to let him renege on their agreement just because the man was suddenly uncomfortable.

"You'll regret hearing this, boy."

"Better that than regretting not hearing it."

Mitsugu pursed his lips in consternation, but after a few moments, he began to speak, albeit reluctantly. "Fine, then. But no questions. I wouldn't be able to answer them anyway," he said firmly, then looked away.

No—he was still looking in Tatsuya's direction, but his eyes were focused elsewhere, on some place—or some time—far in the distance.

And then Mitsugu's long recollection began.

It was eighteen years ago.

We of the Yotsuba clan had received news we had been desperately wanting to hear:

Miya was pregnant. We all immediately gathered here at the main house, our family's home, to await the delivery of her child.

At the time, the tragedy of 2062 was still fresh in our minds—the loathsome memory of Maya being kidnapped by Dahan and used as a subject in their experiments. The memory of the wrenching cost of our revenge: thirty core members of the family, dead.

But a new generation was coming. That alone was cause for joy. We wanted to be considerate toward Maya, who had lost the ability to bear children, but Maya celebrated her sister's news more than anyone else. Could it be that the bond between them, which had been broken by the incident, would be repaired by the birth of a son—a nephew—related to both by blood? Even if things didn't go back to the way they had been, perhaps we would once again see the twins getting along the way they once had. Or so we hoped.

At any rate, the knowledge that new life was growing within Miya had us all overjoyed.

In addition to the superior genes that came from her spouse, who had been chosen after painstaking calculation, Miya was the most talented mental interference magician in the world. It was expected that any offspring of hers would naturally be a superior magician—nobody doubted this.

But our hopes and ambitions went much further than that.

Miya's specialty was a magic only she could perform: mental structure interference. The ability to alter the state of the mind itself.

The older the target of mental structure interference, the worse the possible side effects. However, with a child whose sense of self was yet undeveloped, the side effects of mental structure interference were lessened.

So given a fetus whose sense of self wasn't only undeveloped but nonexistent, it stood to reason that there was no limit to how much its mind could be altered or how much power it could be granted. Such fantasies seemed to arise spontaneously in our minds.

The atrocity we had suffered made us obsessed. We were obsessed with creating a guardian for the family who would possess absolute, overwhelming power. The clan would birth a transcendent figure, a magician to best all other magicians, who would never allow tragedy to again befall us.

Be our enemy another nation, or the entire world itself, we of the Yotsuba would be protected from any oppression. We would possess absolute power. This magician's power would keep the whole world at bay. And it would be the magic technology of the Yotsuba that would bring about such a being. This was our dream.

The entire family was consumed by this ambition. It wasn't that each of us individually hoped to see this being created but that the obsession lurked in the collective heart of the family as a whole.

Mitsugu's cup was empty. Irritated, he rang the service bell with a certain vehemence. When the housekeeper hurried over, he ordered her to refill his tea and to bring a pitcher of water as well. While the housekeeper was away fetching his request, he sat in stony-faced silence.

Only after they were alone again did Mitsugu continue.

We visited Miya constantly under the pretenses of wishing her well, and we prayed for the child within her.

We prayed that the child would grow strong. Strong enough to turn back all the villainy and prejudice of the world.

And we prayed that that power would be used to protect our own children. That the child would be an infallible guardian, able to forestall any misfortune and protect against any tragedy.

This selfish wish we not only held in our hearts but also sometimes spoke aloud.

Miya would smile as she listened to our selfish hopes. She would smile and say, "I hope to bear you such a child."

Miya's mental structure interference would enable her to make the child in her womb into such a person. Our prayers, we thought, were meant to help her do so.

Maya also frequently came to visit Miya. She didn't fall to her knees and pray the way we did, but as she conversed with her twin, I remember her gaze sometimes falling lovingly upon her sister's growing belly.

Mitsugu paused his reminiscence.

He poured water from the pitcher into a glass.

His hand was faintly trembling.

After draining the glass, he remained silent for a time. Tatsuya noticed him start to open his mouth several times, but his trembling lips seemed to be having trouble forming words.

Eventually, though, after Mitsugu emptied a second glass of water in a single long drink, he managed to collect himself and continue.

But despite what she said, that was not Miya's true aim. We learned as much about nine months later.

Miya's true wish was to avenge herself. Her dearest desire was for someone with the power to take that revenge. She wanted to give birth to someone who could stand in judgment of the world that had wounded her and Maya so deeply.

Even as she appeared to hope for a child who would protect the entire family, in her heart of hearts she nurtured a child of vengeance, who would be able to annihilate any and all who stood against her.

Not a single one of us realized this truth. Not a single one of us saw the way she had split her heart into two, nor understood the depths of her suffering.

Mitsugu focused his gaze on Tatsuya's face, then spoke. "And then you were born. You, with the power she gave you—the power to bring ruin to the world."

His breathing was ragged, and he was obviously disturbed. "How could anyone judge a newborn child? you might well ask. But we knew. Even then, we knew."

Tatsuya was about to suggest a break on the man's behalf, but Mitsugu continued, a man possessed. Once again, his attention returned to the past.

My uncle, the late Eisaku Yotsuba, the former head of the family, had the ability to analyze another person's magic-calculation region and measure their latent potential for magic. The techniques the Yotsuba family uses to analyze magic-calculation regions are largely derived from his work.

Eisaku performed such an analysis on Miya's newborn son. We were all breathless with anticipation to hear his estimation of the infant's capacity.

I remember his words to this very day.

This is what my uncle said:

"This child has the power to destroy the world."

He had the power to break down all material or information bodies, as well as the power to restore any material or information body as long as it was within twenty-four hours. As long as he didn't die, he even had the power to recover, and to revive, others.

This was not what we had all hoped for, but it was not incompatible, either.

The power to destroy anything: We had wished for the power to protect an individual from the prejudice of the world. This was the power to annihilate that prejudice.

The power to restore anything: This was the power to nullify the wounds of anyone he'd failed to protect.

Finally, the power to never fall. This was an essential ability for any who would make an enemy of the whole world and face it alone. The child could face endless replenished armies, but with this power, he would never need reinforcements.

Hearing Eisaku's pronouncement, we finally understood what it was that we had so dearly wished for and what this single life had been twisted into.

It was a demon who possessed the power to end the world. That was what the Yotsuba clan's twisted prayers had brought into being. It was the embodiment of our deeply held conviction that as long as the Yotsuba clan was safe, the rest of the world could burn.

The newborn had committed no sin. In fact, it was a victim. But we were terribly conflicted over whether the infant our sin had created should be allowed to live.

The child had the power to destroy the world. Magic can run wild when its user experiences extreme emotions—even if they never had any intent to do so, it was possible that the child might one day actually do something irreparable.

The heads of all the branch families and their heirs assembled to discuss the matter at length. I don't remember for how many days and nights we talked. It's hard to tell whether it lasted three days or a month. But as the heir to the Kuroba family, I was there.

And in the end, we came to the conclusion that the child had to die. No—had to be killed.

All of us from the meeting came to Eisaku and delivered our conclusion. "We must kill the child immediately."

* * *

Mitsugu's gaze had been downcast, but then he paused and looked Tatsuya in the eye. He wore an exhausted smile on his face.

"It was my father, Juuzou Kuroba, who represented the Kuroba family when the branch families went to deliver their pronouncement that the infant—you—should be killed. I was not opposed."

Tatsuya said nothing, because he had been told at the start that his questions would not be answered. He merely waited quietly for the story to continue.

Mitsugu interpreted this silence as shock. "I suppose this is enough to shock even you, eh?" He chuckled, thinking it a display of humanity. "You weren't killed, though, because Eisaku rejected our proposal."

Mitsugu sank, his head lolling down as though his neck had lost the strength to keep it steady. It was a strangely doll-like motion.

Eisaku told us to think rationally, rather than wallow in our shame.

He explained that however accidentally, we had gained the power to destroy the world. It was a trump card for the Yotsuba family, he said.

Eisaku's determination was that it would be an awful waste to throw away this power over our self-indulgent feelings of guilt—and to add infanticide to the list of our crimes in the process.

"Tatsuya" would be raised to be the finest combat magician possible. Because of his simultaneous capacity for dismantling and regeneration, he would be unable to use other magic. In order to protect himself in battle without the use of magic and increase his survivability no matter what circumstances he found himself in, he would be drilled in the most advanced combat techniques. And to make sure his emotions always stayed in check, his capacity to feel them at all would be deeply restricted. This was Eisaku's decision as the head of the family.

"Since birth, you have been given everything possible to mold you into a warrior. As soon as you could stand, you began rigorous physical training. Eisaku was serious. He wanted you to be useful. He was the one who saved you from death, after all."

Mitsugu murmured the words, his head still hanging limply. Tatsuya could tell that he was no longer speaking about the past but rather addressing him, Tatsuya, directly. Mitsugu had unwittingly turned Eisaku Yotsuba's decision into his and the rest of the family's absolution.

Satisfied with this clarification, Mitsugu again sank into himself.

As soon as he could walk, his combat training began. No matter how much he wailed and cried, the boy's desires were ignored. Isolated from the very family he should have been able to rely upon, he soon abandoned any resistance. Or perhaps he merely buried any feelings of defiance deep within himself. And his training continued at a pace far from normal.

Beginning with learning to dispatch wild animals without the use of ranged weapons, his training partners changed from military dogs to enhanced tactical animals—and finally to living soldiers.

"After Eisaku passed away, Maya became the new head of the family. Shortly thereafter, Maya and Miya made you the subject of an artificial magician experiment. It, and you, were deemed a grand success, and you were appointed Miyuki's Guardian."

Mitsugu finally looked up and began conversing normally. "But even after that, your combat training continued—until your formative years came and it was determined that the excessive training would adversely affect your development."

"That much I remember."

In fact, Tatsuya had clear memories going back before the artificial magician experiment, but they didn't feel real to him. Memories before the experiment felt like watching a movie.

"I suppose you would. You were six by then."

Mitsugu's voice was hoarse. He seemed to suddenly remember

the pitcher of water and refilled his glass, then drained half of it. "After Eisaku died, your training continued. Miya didn't do anything to intervene. And why would she? She needed you alive in order to eventually carry out her vengeance."

He drank the remaining water in the glass.

"You are the embodiment of Miya's enmity toward the world and the symbol of the Yotsuba family's great sin: our simpleminded wish for a superman to do our bidding and our failure to understand the rage and sorrow of one woman."

Mitsugu's grief seemed to almost sing—an awful song, a curse on both Tatsuya and himself.

"Knowing what you were, we could not allow you to remain at the center of the family. You couldn't be allowed to inherit the Yotsuba family influence, and you had to be kept away from the National Defense Forces. We did not want to compound our sins."

With that, Mitsugu seemed disinclined to say anything further. Tatsuya inferred that his story had ended.

"I understand, then."

"If that is indeed so, then you should immediately resign as Miyuki's Guardian. You must know that she will accept whatever you say."

Tatsuya smiled coldly and shook his head. "What I understand is that the motivation behind your seemingly inexplicable actions is mere self-indulgent guilt."

"What?!" Mitsugu slammed his fist into the arm of the chair he sat in.

A variety of methods by which he might kill Mitsugu flashed through Tatsuya's mind.

"You told me what I wanted to know, as you promised you would. I'd like to excuse myself, now. Will that be all?"

"...Go, then. I have no more business with you." Mitsugu rang the handbell.

The same housekeeper who had led Tatsuya in appeared. Mitsugu ordered her to show him to the door and out of the house.

At 6:50 PM, Tatsuya and Miyuki were led to the inner dining room by Minami. During the dinner itself, Minami stood at their side to wait on them.

Fumiya, Ayako, and Yuuka were already seated by the time Tatsuya and Miyuki arrived in the dining room. Miyuki was seated at the far end of the table, across from Fumiya, and Tatsuya next to her, across from Ayako. Next to Miyuki, at the end of the table, was Maya's place. Miyuki had clearly been seated in the position of the highest honor, second only to Maya.

One minute before 7:00 PM, Katsushige Shibata arrived in the dining hall. Just as Tatsuya had suspected, this meant that all the candidates for succession were present—but he still didn't understand why he himself was there. Ayako was Fumiya's assistant, not his bodyguard, so it made sense that she was next to him. But as far as the Yotsuba family was concerned, Tatsuya was merely Miyuki's Guardian and nothing more.

Katsushige came unescorted to the table. Not even Kotona, who was always at his side, was with him, to say nothing of Kanata.

But Tatsuya seemed to be the only one who found his presence at the table odd. Miyuki, of course, did not. But strangely neither Fumiya, Ayako, Yuuka, nor even Katsushige seemed to harbor any curiosity about finding themselves around the same table as their black sheep relative.

But he was underestimating his own importance, and he was underestimating the other magicians at the table, too.

The five other people present all regarded him as a magician who possessed equivalent or greater strength than they did. It was obvious to them that he would sit at the same table as they did. But Tatsuya nevertheless felt distinctly uncomfortable, as he had no idea that they were so broad-minded.

The clock struck seven.

The doors at the far end of the dining room opened, revealing the entrance that was for the exclusive use of the head of the Yotsuba family.

Escorted by the head butler, Hayama, Maya emerged through the portal wearing a long dress whose dark red color was near black.

Everybody stood. Tatsuya pushed back his own chair, but servants behind the five others pulled out their high-backed chairs for them. Minami, of course, took care of Miyuki's chair.

"In spite of the rather sudden invitation, I bid you all welcome. Please, sit," said Maya, gracefully seating herself in the chair that Hayama had pulled out for her.

Once Maya was seated and settled, the six other attendees all took their seats.

"First, let us have dinner. Katsushige, Yuuka—if you would like, I can have some wine brought out for you."

Yuuka and Katsushige exchanged a quick glance.

It was Yuuka who answered first. "I appreciate the offer, but I'll have to abstain. I'm not much of a drinker."

"Come to think of it, Yuuka, you don't have much tolerance for alcohol, do you?" said Maya with a generous smile.

"No, as embarrassing as that is to admit," Yuuka replied smartly.

Maya turned her gaze to Katsushige. "What about you? You look like you'd have quite the constitution."

"I'm afraid looks are deceptive in this case... I tend to have terrible hangovers. So with apologies, given that I'll need to save my strength for tomorrow's event, I'll have to refrain tonight."

"You don't need to be quite so formal, you know. Forcing people to drink isn't one of my vices." Maya smiled pleasantly, then raised her hand, giving Hayama, behind her, a signal.

At a glance from Hayama, the servers all retreated, then immediately returned with hors d'oeuvres.

"As tomorrow's celebration will feature traditional Japanese New Year's dishes, I chose Western-style courses for tonight's dinner. I hope you'll enjoy them." Maya slid her knife through the terrine appetizer in front of her and brought a bite to her ruby-red lips.

All present picked up their knives and forks, and the meal began.

The cuisine was generally French, although not rigorously so. Maya seemed not to feel any need to hew to formality—one example was the duck that was brought out instead of the seafood that more a traditional setting might have suggested.

When she finished the sherbet that came after that course, Maya adjusted her position in her seat, causing everyone else, Tatsuya included, to straighten in their chairs attentively.

"Now then, I suppose we ought to get to business." She looked over the assembled six and smiled serenely. "Katsushige, Yuuka, Miyuki, Fumiya." She addressed the four succession candidates in descending order of age. "You are the four remaining candidates being considered for the position of Yotsuba family head. At tomorrow's New Year's celebration, I will announce my successor."

All six of the gathered—not just the four candidates—watched Maya carefully. Somewhere along the line, all of the servants had left the room, save Hayama.

"However, suddenly hearing the pronouncement in front of everyone hardly leaves any time for you to process your emotions. Given that, I have decided to inform those at this table ahead of time."

It was Miyuki who was most obviously nervous at this. Katsushige and Yuuka, as well as Fumiya and Ayako for some reason, all seemed quite calm.

Surprisingly, it was Fumiya who interrupted Maya as she was about to deliver her decision. "If I might, ma'am, there's something I'd like to say."

"My goodness, Fumiya. Do go on."

"With your permission, then," he said, standing. He gave a nervous bow, then continued. "I, Fumiya Kuroba of the Kuroba family, formally withdraw my candidacy for succession and recommend Miyuki Shiba to be named successor."

Fumiya bowed again to Maya, then took his seat.

"Hmm. How very interesting."

For Fumiya to formally withdraw his candidacy after Maya had stated that her decision was already final was, by a certain definition, a kind of defiance.

But Maya made no move to remonstrate him. Instead, she regarded Fumiya's decision to choose this moment, of all times, to withdraw with great interest.

"Ma'am, if you would, I would also like to speak."

"Yuuka. Don't tell me, you too?" Maya asked with a smile.

"Yes." Yuuka stood and made a show of bowing. "The Tsukuba family also recommends that Miyuki Shiba be named successor."

She bowed again and sat, as Maya looked on with an amused smile.

"Did someone put the idea into your heads that you couldn't just let the main family decide the successor all on its own?" she said, dabbing at the corners of her eyes with a handkerchief as she looked back and forth between Fumiya and Yuuka.

"No, nothing of the sort—"

Hearing Fumiya speak, Ayako smoothly cut in and explained their position. "Please forgive me butting in, ma'am, but it is entirely Fumiya's and my own determination that Miyuki is the most suitable to succeed you. Our father fully respects Fumiya's feelings and agrees with his decision to withdraw his candidacy. It is not at all our intention to raise any objection to your decision."

"I see… So in other words, without any connection to the New Year's celebration or the events in the days leading up to it, the Kuroba family has decided to support Miyuki as the next successor. Do I have that right?"

It was Fumiya who answered the question Maya put to them. "Yes. That is entirely correct."

Maya chuckled. "Such filial piety, Fumiya."

Fumiya's design—and therefore, Mitsugu's, as the figure pushing him—was transparent to Maya. The branch families' attempt to delay Miyuki's appointment by preventing her from attending the celebrations had failed. Even if the Kuroba family hadn't been directly involved, they had obviously been part of the obstructionist faction.

And now they were trying to preemptively draw attention away from their mutinous stance. But since Maya was not particularly inclined to condemn the families involved with the interdiction operation—because she knew it would end in failure—this little intrigue was meaningless.

"I wonder why the Tsukuba family chose this particular timing to announce their withdrawal from consideration?" Maya mused with a piercing gaze.

Yuuka met her eyes with a flash of irritation. "Well, ma'am, if we didn't speak up now, we wouldn't have another chance, would we?"

"You mean you wouldn't have another chance to make sure Miyuki owed you a favor?"

"Not to put too fine a point on it, but no. The Tsukuba family wants to have established a record of having immediately supported the successor. To be frank, our family has fallen behind the Kuroba and Shibata families, in terms of power."

Even Maya couldn't help but smile awkwardly at this exceedingly blunt statement.

"Personally, I don't think that a family's power is determined solely by its direct combat ability...but I do understand the Tsukuba family's perspective. Miyuki, it looks like Yuuka is hoping to gain your favor."

Miyuki looked momentarily surprised to be suddenly addressed but was certainly not some easily flustered little girl. "Well, at the moment, I am merely another candidate for succession...but I share my aunt's view that combat ability is not the sole measure of a magician's worth."

Maya gave Miyuki a nod as though to say *well done*.

She then turned her attention to Katsushige. "Now then, Katsushige. Before I announce my decision, since we seem to be in a democratic sort of mood... What are your thoughts?"

Without standing, Katsushige straightened his posture and shifted in his chair to face Maya. "Ma'am. If the Kuroba and Tsukuba families are firm in their resolution to back Miyuki, then the Shibata family has no objection. I have received confirmation of this from our family head, Osamu."

"I see. So you're willing to abide by the majority."

"Yes." Katsushige nodded, without betraying the slightest acknowledgment that he himself had directly interfered with Miyuki's arrival. He was so dignified that even if Maya had decided to interrogate him here, face-to-face, he would have been able to protest his ignorance with perfect composure.

"However, should we withdraw our candidacy for succession, there is something we would ask of you."

"A quid pro quo, you mean?" Maya's eyes narrowed. Her expression didn't go as far as seeming openly suspicious, but it certainly wasn't a pleased one, either. Or perhaps she was simply irritated at Katsushige's insistence on saying nothing about his family's obstruction.

"Not at all." Katsushige responded decisively. "Merely a request."

Maya's expression shifted. "Oh?"

"As I have nothing to offer the new family head, there is nothing to be exchanged."

"How straightforward and honest of you. Very well then, let's hear it. What is it that you would ask of me?"

"I would ask that you give your blessing for a marriage between me, Katsushige Shibata, and Kotona Tsutsumi."

Yuuka choked mid-sip of water.

Fumiya's face faintly flushed, the excitement still a bit too much for him.

"Kotona...your Guardian, correct?"

"Yes."

Maya looked thoughtful. "One of the second-generation Bard series, as I recall. The Bard series are still a bit genetically unstable, so I'm not sure she would be the best choice for the wife of a branch family head."

"That is what my father said, as well."

"You wouldn't be satisfied with her as your mistress?"

Maya's words had a far greater effect on Fumiya, who was trapped between her and Katsushige, than they did on Katsushige himself. He turned bright red and looked straight down. Beside him, Ayako seemed entirely unflustered, so his reaction was either thanks to the difference in age, gender, or disposition.

"You're already in a common-law relationship, aren't you?"

"You're well-informed," Katsushige offered, his composure unruffled.

"The thing is… Guardians are supposed to be the protectors of the clan's most important magical assets, which is part of why we normally assign women as Guardians. But I wonder if your Guardian is merely an excuse for you to keep Kotona Tsutsumi at your side?"

"That is not the *only* reason," he replied, trying to argue for the utility of Kotona's magical abilities, but after a look from Maya, he quickly corrected himself. "No, you're right." Given that his primary goal here was to keep Kotona by his side, there was no advantage in muddying the waters.

"Hmm…" Maya placed a hand to her cheek and struck a contemplative pose. It was a fair impression of a person deep in thought, but nobody else at the table believed for a minute that she was actually agonizing over her decision.

"I hardly want to tear a pair of lovers apart," she said, then for some reason looked to Miyuki. "And just because she's an engineered magician doesn't mean she'll necessarily die young." Maya returned her gaze to Katsushige.

Miyuki noticed Maya's look but had no idea what it meant. It occurred to her that Maya might be referring to Honami or Minami, but that didn't quite make sense. She was frustrated at the lack of clarity, but she couldn't very well demand Maya explain the meaning of a single fleeting glance.

Whether or not Maya noticed Miyuki's frustration, she was watching Katsushige closely. As he nervously waited for her answer, she finally broke into a pleasant smile.

"Very well. If you'd become the main family head, your personal desires wouldn't be the only factor in your marriage."

Miyuki flinched. Tatsuya gave her a worried look, but Miyuki's gaze was frozen as she stared down at her hands.

Maya merely glanced briefly at Miyuki before returning to her conversation with Katsushige. "However, with branch family heads, there's less need to be so calculating. If you will step down from being considered for succession, I will speak to Osamu."

"Thank you." Katsushige stood and lowered his head in a deep bow. When he looked up, Maya gestured for him to sit back down.

She then exhaled a sigh. "Goodness, it rather feels like I don't need to say this, now, but…" Her relaxed expression stiffened. "Miyuki, I am naming you the next family head."

Miyuki answered stiffly, "…I understand."

"Fortunately, everyone here seems to have endorsed you, so take heart, and know that you have no need to be self-conscious about it."

"Yes, Aunt Maya. I will do my very best."

Miyuki stood and directed a formal bow first to Maya and then to the table. The fact that she was seated opposite Katsushige, and therefore appeared to be bowing to him, was only a perverse coincidence.

"Now then, shall we return to our meal?" Maya asked, whereupon Hayama clapped twice.

The main course meat dish—though incorrect according to a strict interpretation of fine dining norms—was brought out, and thereafter, the table was filled with idle, friendly chatter.

But once the dinner was over, Maya directed Tatsuya and Miyuki to remain.

When everyone else had left, the table setting was cleared. A cup of black tea was set in front of Maya. Tatsuya received black coffee; his sister, coffee with milk.

The servants, Hayama included, retreated.

Maya took a sip of her tea, then addressed the pair in a pleasant tone.

"Miyuki, first of all, congratulations. And, Tatsuya, I know you went through quite a bit of trouble, too."

"Thank you very much, Aunt Maya."

"Yes, thank you."

Tatsuya and Miyuki both bowed from their seats. Neither of them had touched their cups.

"Now, I asked you to stay because I have something very important to discuss with you."

Tatsuya could feel Miyuki stiffen next to him.

"As I said before, when you become family head, the choice of whom you marry is no longer yours alone."

"—I understand." Miyuki's hands gripped her thighs.

"But before we get into that... Tatsuya."

Tatsuya had not expected to be addressed here, but he let none of the confusion he felt creep into his response. "Yes?"

"You may have trouble believing what I'm about to tell you, but... Miyuki is not your biological sister."

Miyuki gave a sharp gasp—a cry, really, that stayed unvoiced. She covered her hand with her mouth, and wide-eyed, she froze, looking almost like a marble statue.

But *frozen* was not the most appropriate term to describe her in that moment. It was true that she was not moving, but her wide eyes seemed to swirl with flames of complicated emotion.

Compared with Miyuki, Tatsuya appeared to be less disturbed, but that was merely because his emotions had exceeded his ability to process them. He took the shock he couldn't process, detached it from himself, transfigured it into an objective, disinterested thought, and spat it back out at Maya.

"As expected, I don't believe you. There is, after all, overwhelming evidence that Miyuki and I are biological siblings."

Maya smiled an unworried smile at the suddenly emotionless Tatsuya. "And yet, it's true. You see, Tatsuya—

"—You are my son."

The shocking statement was enough to stun even Tatsuya into silence.

"Tatsuya, you are my son, born from an egg I cryogenically preserved before the incident, artificially fertilized, and carried to term by a surrogate—my sister. Your father, of course, is not Tatsuro. This makes Miyuki your cousin."

It's impossible.

Those were the words that first shot through Tatsuya's mind when he regained the ability to think.

It's impossible for Miyuki to be my cousin.
It's impossible for Miyuki to be anything other than my sister.

As doubt crept in, shame came on its heels, but Tatsuya let none of these emotions show on his face.

"...I would like to hear more details later, if that's all right."

Maya responded to Tatsuya's request with her usual airiness. "Certainly. I can see how it would be difficult to accept right away. We'll have a nice mother-son chat after this, just the two of us." She gave a satisfied nod, then turned to Miyuki. "Now, about what I mentioned before. As the head of the Yotsuba family, you unfortunately aren't free to pursue just any romantic relationship."

"I understand." Miyuki's expression was still stiff, but there was a sliver of hope that crept into her tone. Her hands shook in her lap, not out of sadness but out of delight at the premonition of something so perfect she barely dared to hope for it.

"Tomorrow, when I announce the successor, I will also be announcing your fiancé. Who will be—"

Miyuki gasped faintly—and it was only faint because she was already holding her breath.

"—Tatsuya."

Miyuki clapped both her hands over her mouth, where they stayed, trembling.

Once she had stifled her cry, she brought her hands down to her chest.

There she pressed them to her heart, squeezing her eyes closed and hunching over as though she were bearing some terrible pain.

She was experiencing firsthand the meaning of phrase *feeling like your heart might burst.*

But not from sadness—from joy. A joy so strong it felt like its own sort of pain.

Miyuki was happy, so happy, and her heart soared so high she thought she might go crazy, but with great effort, she calmed herself and brought her face back up.

Both her eyes welled up, and she looked like she might burst into tears at any moment.

Maya did not scold her niece for her outburst. "Tatsuya, I'll need you to attend tomorrow's celebration, since I will be presenting you as Miyuki's fiancé. And that's everything I had to say."

Miyuki looked slowly down. Teardrops fell from her eyes to land on her hands, which rested on her knees.

"Miyuki, tomorrow will be your engagement party. It's a big

moment for you, so take the rest of today to make sure you're ready to look your best."

"Thank you… Oh, thank you…" Miyuki answered, doing her best to hold back her sobs, her head still lowered.

Maya regarded her with a gaze that could only be called maternal, though there was a flash of something cold in her eyes. "Hayama."

Hayama quickly appeared at the sound. "Yes, madam."

As he did so, Tatsuya was helping Miyuki to her feet and drying her eyes with a handkerchief.

"Please call for Minami. And have some servants prepare Miyuki's bath."

"Very well, madam."

Minami soon arrived, and Maya briskly delivered her instructions. "Minami, take Miyuki to her room. You'll be contacted once her bath is drawn, and once it is, escort her there."

"Yes, ma'am."

Minami led Miyuki to the guest rooms.

Maya turned to face Tatsuya. "Let's change our venue as well, shall we?"

"Of course."

Maya stood.

Hayama opened the door.

Tatsuya followed Maya.

As Tatsuya passed by, Hayama gave him a deep, respectful bow. It was the biggest change in his reception here that Tatsuya had yet seen.

Maya led Tatsuya to her study. It was his first time in the room. In fact, since Maya's ascension to head of the family, the only people to enter the room aside from Maya and Hayama had been HAR maintenance engineers and furniture delivery workers. It was more accurate to say that he was only the second person she'd ever invited into the room with her.

The study had a large, sturdy desk with a high-backed chair, floor-to-ceiling bookshelves, and a vintage couch and coffee table set. Hayama gestured for Tatsuya to sit on the sofa, which he did. Maya sat on its opposite end, and as Tatsuya scanned the room, she spoke to him in a warm, familiar tone.

"What are you looking at, Tatsuya?"

"Ah, pardon me. I was just realizing that when you call Miyuki on the phone, you're not calling from your study."

"You notice the most curious things." Maya chuckled.

"So this is an entirely off-line environment, then?"

"Yes."

Maya's answer was not accurate. There was one machine in the room with a single network connection. But it was not a total lie, either, as that one line was completely independent, and the only data coming out of this room were search keys that ran through one particular device, so it was a half-truth.

"Do you take your coffee black, sir?"

Tatsuya felt deeply uncomfortable at being called *sir* by Hayama, but he knew that wasn't what he needed to be thinking about.

"Yes, black, please," he said in as natural a voice as he could manage.

Coffee was placed in front of Tatsuya, while Maya received herbal tea.

Tatsuya was concerned that the scent of his coffee would overpower the scent of the herbal tea, but he decided that wasn't his problem to solve and so said nothing. He waited for Maya to bring her cup to her lips first, then took a sip of the coffee in turn.

To his immense chagrin, he had to admit that it was better than the coffee Miyuki made.

"This is delicious. You'll pardon me for saying so, Hayama, but you've outdone yourself."

"I'm honored that you would say so, sir. Truth be told, I cheated a bit."

"You cheated?"

"Yes. I'm embarrassed to admit I borrowed the help of a bit of magic."

"I'm no match for Hayama when it comes to subtle little uses of magic like that," added Maya amusedly, seeing Tatsuya's openly surprised expression. "The magic of magic really is in how you use it."

"You flatter me too much. I am merely using what abilities I have in the service of my chosen profession."

Hayama's simple statement invited deep contemplation, but Tatsuya resisted the temptation and instead turned to face Maya.

Maya seemed to have been waiting for this signal to speak about the matter at hand. She returned her cup to its saucer and met Tatsuya's gaze.

"Well, then… Where shall we begin?"

"First, may I say something?" Tatsuya seized the opportunity.

Maya seemed to have been expecting this. "Goodness, what could it be?" She put a hand to her mouth and widened her eyes in a show of mock surprise, but the curl at the corners of her mouth—a smile that she deliberately revealed—made it clear that she wasn't seriously trying to fake a reaction.

"Why would you tell such a lie?" His eyes narrowed, not in irritation at her childish display but rather in simple suspicion.

"What lie?" Her tone was openly brazen.

Tatsuya didn't let his anger or frustration show. "The lie that Miyuki is not my sister," he said in a tone that could only be described as pleasant. A tone that was simply speaking the truth, without need for emphasis or volume.

Yet Maya disputed that truth. "Why, it's not a lie," she said, in a tone every bit as light as Tatsuya's.

Tatsuya stared at his aunt's face, not understanding what she was so confidently self-satisfied about.

Maya took a leisurely sip of her herbal tea. "You said there was overwhelming evidence that you and she are biological siblings, but what really constitutes proof?" she asked with deliberate patience, setting her cup down and looking Tatsuya in the eyes almost reproachfully.

There was no laughter in her voice, but her expression was quite amused, and there was a savage gleam that flickered in her eyes.

"Family registries? We can manipulate those however we like. DNA tests? The results are just documents that the hospital sends. You didn't conduct the test yourself, did you, Tatsuya?" Maya's lips curled into a crescent. "The family only knows about what happened after my sister's pregnancy. They don't know a thing about what might have happened before."

"Aunt Maya." Tatsuya's voice was unmoved. Like a vast, inexorable ingot of red-hot iron, it erased the condescending expression from the woman's face. "Just who do you think I am?"

Now it was Maya's turn to be stunned into silence.

"I can recognize the composition and configuration of matter, and I have the ability to break it down into arbitrary previous states. Being able to recognize the compositional elements of matter means that I can also recognize what they arose from."

"I believe your informational retroaction is limited to twenty-four hours, though."

"The compositional information is contained in the matter as it currently exists. There's no need to look back in time."

Maya's and Hayama's expressions were united in betraying how unforeseen this revelation was for them, but their underlying emotions were different. Maya's face had a flustered *Oops…!* quality to it, whereas Hayama was simply astonished.

"So I know. I can tell that my body and Miyuki's body share the same physical origins. My body and Miyuki's body were created with sperm from the same man and eggs from the same woman."

When she spoke, Maya's murmuring voice was tinged with surrender. "You really aren't like other humans, arc you?"

"It's very kind of you to say so."

"It wasn't a compliment."

Maya smiled a baffled sort of smile, her eyes drifting down to her teacup. In the end she didn't reach for it and simply looked back up to Tatsuya.

"Fine, then. I acknowledge it.

"What I said earlier was a lie.

"You were not conceived with my egg, and you are indeed my sister's child."

Maya delivered her confession unapologetically, and after hearing it, Tatsuya sighed. "Then why the lie?"

"It's also not entirely a lie to say that you and Miyuki are not biological siblings."

Maya's response was not an answer to his question, but it contained something Tatsuya wanted to hear the end of, so he waited for her to continue.

"You see, Miyuki was engineered."

Tatsuya's eyes widened. His breath caught, and for a moment, he couldn't speak. "...Do you mean to tell me that she was genetically manipulated? But—she hasn't had any symptoms of—"

"And yet, it's the truth. The reason Miyuki hasn't shown any instability or defects is because she is a fully engineered magician—a gem without flaws. The masterpiece of the Yotsuba family."

"Why—?"

"Why was she made? Why, she was made for you, Tatsuya."

Tatsuya was dumbfounded. His consciousness was bleached blank by the sheer impossibility of the idea.

"Your power is something that could never be allowed to slip out of your control. It's something that needs a way to be stopped at any cost. My sister probably could have done it. Her mental structure interference magic had the ability to temporarily close a gate in the subconscious mind of a target. But you would obviously outlive her, so a magician was created who would always be by your side and always be able to stop you—Miyuki."

Maya's gaze as she looked into Tatsuya's eyes was so serious it was almost frightening.

"Miyuki is an engineered magician created with one purpose: to stop you."

"Miyuki is…for me? Not me, for her?" Tatsuya murmured in shock. He didn't even notice the logical error hiding in his words.

"That's right. Miyuki is a girl who was born just for you." Maya's expression and tone both softened. "I mean, do you really think a girl so beautiful could ever have been born naturally? No such perfect complexion, such exquisite symmetry, could ever come to be incidentally."

Maya smiled wryly, realizing she'd allowed a note of envy to slip into her voice. "Of course, I don't imagine that following the same procedure again would produce a girl like Miyuki. In a way, her beauty is a miracle, numinous, surpassing anything humans or nature could hope to recreate."

"…Does she know about this?" Tatsuya asked.

Maya shook her head slowly. "No. Miyuki has never been told this, nor have any of the branch family heads. The only people who ever knew were the late family head Eisaku, my late sister, myself, Hayama, Kurebayashi, who manages the engineering facility, and Kurebayashi's former boss, who managed the engineering facility at the time."

She paused, then continued in a gentle voice. "Tatsuya…the bond between you and Miyuki is stronger than a parent and child, but from a genetic standpoint, you are much more closely related to me than you are to her." Her voice sounded almost pleading. "And when I said you were my son, that wasn't a complete lie, either."

"But—"

Maya cut off Tatsuya's objection with a honeyed, sticky-sweet voice. "It's true that genetically we are nephew and aunt. But psychologically, Tatsuya, you are my son."

"Psychologically?"

"When my uncles and Mitsugu and the rest of them first learned about your power, they despaired, then they were terrified. But I was happy. I wanted to dance with joy. It was hard to keep myself from shouting, I was so delighted. After all, your magic could make my fondest wish come true."

As she recalled the memory, Maya almost trembled, her expression rapturous. "Your magic could turn the Earth into a planet of death. It could destroy civilization. It could wreak vengeance upon this world—this cruel world, that in its cruelty stole from me both past and future, that tore my one sliver of happiness as a woman from me."

Maya's curse from the grudge she bore against the world mingled with her sweet tone.

"It's not a lie that I'm your mother. It wasn't my sister who wished for your birth. It was my hope that you be brought into the world. That was Mitsugu and his faction's great misunderstanding. It was my wish, my prayer that you destroy the world, and it was you who were born in answer to my heart's desire. It was my sister in whose womb you grew, but it was I who created your magic to be as it is. As a magician, you are very much my son."

"But, Aunt Maya," Tatsuya managed hoarsely, "I thought you weren't able to use mental interference magic?"

That didn't slow Maya down at all. "You're right. That's why it was a miracle. My desire overturned even the rules of magic and made something impossible happen. Perhaps it's because we were twins, my sister and I. We were twins, so my will was able to work through my sister's magic. Perhaps the prayers I offered you were stronger even than my sister's bond with her own child, twisting the power of my sister's magic to making my hopes a reality."

Maya's voice was feverish—because she herself was caught up in a fever.

"And my sister knew this. She knew that somehow I, her younger sister, had seized control of her womb. She stole from me my very self, and I stole from her, her son. Awful sisters, weren't we?"

Even in self-reproach, her voice was excited and sweet.

"And still my sister tried her best to love you. In the end, she couldn't do it, but please know that she did try."

Though she was telling Tatsuya to understand his mother, Maya's voice was filled with undisguised contempt for her.

"The artificial magician experiments were carried out to prevent you from becoming emotionally unstable and allowing your magic to explode, so all of the subjects besides you were very literally experimental materials—mere disposable samples. My sister was reluctant to participate right up to the very end, but finally, to avoid you becoming the world's destroyer, the genocide of humanity, evil incarnate, she set her hand to you. By incredible force of will, she was able to steal away only your strongest emotions. It would have been simpler to wipe out your emotions entirely, and the toll it took on her was considerable. But knowing full well it would shorten her lifespan, she tampered with your mind. A mind that my influence had already twisted, she tried to repair, to stave off disaster."

Maya stopped speaking only when she ran out of breath. She didn't even take a sip of tea before continuing.

"In order to keep Miyuki from stopping you, my sister tried to inculcate her with total indifference to you. If Miyuki were indifferent to you, she wouldn't hate you. She would never lose her temper with you. Her emotions would never be the trigger for the sudden detonation of Cocytus, and she would not, in the end, stop you."

It was hard to believe that his mother's cold demeanor had had such deep reasoning behind it. Most likely, anyone other than Tatsuya wouldn't have believed it.

"For the same reason, Miyuki was educated to be a perfect lady, to avoid her becoming emotional and her magic running wild. She was raised to be ever modest and reserved, never becoming hysterical or letting her feelings show too openly. And while it's hard to say we succeeded completely, I don't know that such a perfect lady could ever exist..."

"...Miyuki *is* a perfect lady. Her magic has only ever become uncontrolled because of Oath."

"Oh my," Maya chuckled. "You two really *are* fond of each other, aren't you? I think you'll get along just fine as fiancés."

"Psychology aside, physically we are still undeniably biological siblings. Ordering us to marry is still unreasonable."

"Why is that?"

"I mean..." The problem was so obvious, he had trouble collecting his thoughts.

"If you're worried about genetic defects in the children you might have after marrying her, you needn't. As I said, Miyuki is a fully engineered magician, the epitome of the technological prowess of the Yotsuba. Not only was her body genetically engineered, but her spirit was crafted with the most exquisite mental interference arts. She is the Yotsuba family's greatest achievement, a triumph over every flaw an engineered magician might have, something made by humans but greater than human. There will be no misbegotten children conceived by you and Miyuki. On the honor of the Yotsuba name, I promise that much. There is no factor in her genetic code that could lead to any abnormality."

"But..."

"I doubt she would be upset to learn that she was engineered. She might even be pleased, if she knew the changes meant that, genetically, you and she are too far separated to be considered siblings, since it would mean that there is no barrier whatsoever to her becoming physically intimate with you."

Maya's argument might well have been sound. At the very least,

there weren't any obvious flaws in it that Tatsuya could point out. And in fact, he'd begun to suspect something similar.

Miyuki's body had unmistakably been conceived from germ cells provided by the same parents as Tatsuya.

But there were elements of her that that explanation alone could not account for.

So far as he could perceive, they didn't cause her body any harmful effects, so he'd assumed they were brought about by natural-occurring variation. But now that he was considering them as deliberate alterations, it was a much more logical explanation for the significant difference in compositional elements between he and Miyuki. However reluctantly, he had to admit it.

"Tatsuya, you should tell Miyuki the truth. You should tell her that she was engineered for you, and that at least physically, there are no barriers to your marriage whatsoever."

Tatsuya looked evenly at Maya's face. She returned his gaze but said nothing.

"...All right." Tatsuya finally nodded after a considerable pause. "It's true, this isn't something I should keep silent about."

"It isn't. Keeping her in the dark would wound her terribly."

Maya spoke jokingly, but Tatsuya couldn't deny the truth of what she said.

"Make sure you cherish her," his aunt said, her tone suddenly serious. "If you were ever to lose Miyuki, it would break you. That is how your heart was designed. And broken, you would burn the world to the ground." She spoke like a fortune-teller—or even a prophet. "So keep her close and protect her as long as you live.

"Although, to be honest," Maya suddenly added, "I don't care either way." Her eyes shone more brightly than they had all evening. They blazed with a passionate flame. "If you ever do destroy the world, my heart's thirst for vengeance will be slaked. But if you manage to protect Miyuki from the world's malice, you'll have satisfied my vengeance in a different way. The world that takes such pleasure in trampling on women's lives will have been forced to surrender to a single man."

The flame's name was madness.

"If I could laugh in the face of a pathetic, humbled world just once, I think I would be able to forget what that world did to me." Consumed in a flare of lunacy, Maya smiled an innocent smile. "How lovely, how wonderful that would be. How splendid my son is. You will be the instrument of my vengeance. You will exact the price for little Maya Yotsuba, who died when she was twelve years old."

"Aunt Maya, you are not well."

Tatsuya's words seemed not to reach Maya. Though her ears heard them, her mind did not recognize them. "That is why, Tatsuya, you must take Miyuki as your bride. I will not brook any argument over this."

Hayama came to Maya's side and replaced the now quite cool herbal tea with a fresh, hot cup.

Maya's expression shifted, as if the spirit possessing her had suddenly left her body, and she looked at Tatsuya with eyes unclouded by madness. "Would you like another cup of coffee?"

"No, that's quite all right."

"Really? Oh, goodness, look at the time."

The dinner had ended shortly after nine o'clock, and the clock's hour hand now indicated it was well past ten. Tatsuya himself hadn't noticed, but evidently the thinking he'd done during the conversation's pauses had taken up more time than he'd realized.

"Tomorrow's going to be a busy day, so let's call it a night. Is there anything else you wanted to ask, Tatsuya?"

Tatsuya was wary of rekindling the woman's madness, but there was something he wanted to know, and he wasn't sure if he would get another chance to ask. "As long as you're offering, there is one thing."

"And what's that?"

"Why tomorrow? Is there some reason why you chose tomorrow to announce that I am your son and that Miyuki and I are engaged?"

It was true that the New Year's celebration was the occasion of the largest gathering of all the members of the family. It was well suited for Miyuki's debut as successor. But it occurred to Tatsuya that that alone was a weak reason to choose this moment for the rest of the announcement.

"It wasn't absolutely necessary to do it tomorrow, but yes, I do have a reason." Maya was calm in response to his caution, but she seemed somehow amused, too. "The truth is, I wanted to reveal you as my son this past New Year's Day—but then you had to go and use that magic of yours in such a conspicuous way."

Tatsuya didn't have to ask what the *conspicuous magic* Maya was talking about was—his annihilation of the Great Asian Alliance's naval fleet using Material Burst.

"But at the time the USNA's Stars were moving, so to hide you from their surveillance I'd told you to be on your best behavior—but you wouldn't have it."

"Sorry about that." Tatsuya smiled wryly in spite of himself. It didn't occur to him to believe that that had been her reason for the restriction order, though. It seemed to him an obviously retroactive excuse.

"The past is the past," Maya said with an easy nod. Even with her madness lurking in the shadows, her easy familiarity with Tatsuya hadn't changed.

"Still…after the Stars *tentatively* pulled out of Japan, there was still Kudou-sensei's mental degeneration, and the covert Chinese immortalist, so there was just a bit too much going on."

The mention of General Kudou's mental degeneration had to refer to the Parasidoll incident. The Chinese immortalist was Gongjin Zhou. Considering it all, Tatsuya had to admit it had been an eventful year. Maya's situation notwithstanding, he hadn't really had time to deal with the Yotsubas' internecine conflict.

"So in the end, your debut had to be put off until tomorrow's party."

"I see," said Tatsuya, performing an acceptance of the explanation. He decided that knowing there was no particular necessity behind the choice of tomorrow as the day to announce the lie that he was Maya's son was a gain in and of itself—though the fact was a meaningless one.

"So that really is the end of my explanations." Maya smiled, clearly satisfied with their conversation. She had, after all, managed to convince Tatsuya of what she'd set out to. "Can you find your way back to your room?"

"Yes, *Aunt* Maya," Tatsuya said. "I'll be fine."

"Oh?" she replied, seeming not to notice. "Well, in that case, can I ask you to manage without an escort? I'll have your bath prepared and send someone to call on you in your room when it's ready."

"Understood." Tatsuya took this to mean that the conversation was definitively over. "Thank you for the coffee," he said to Hayama with a bow, then left the study.

After Tatsuya left, Maya remained on the sofa.

"Excellent work, madam," Hayama said from behind her.

"It got a bit more emotional than I'd expected," she replied ruefully. The scene that had just ended had been more exhausting than she'd planned for.

"Given the subject matter, I'm not sure that could have been helped," Hayama offered in an effort to hearten her, but it seemed to only intensify her embarrassment, and she turned her face away in an uncharacteristic pout.

Hayama found this rather amusing, but he was not so unprofessional as to let a smile slip at such a moment. "So this was the plan you'd had at hand all along. I must confess that I'm deeply impressed."

In December of the previous year, immediately after the Yokohama incident, when Maya had called the Shiba siblings to the mansion, she'd told Hayama that she was going to name Miyuki the next Yotsuba family head in order to keep Tatsuya from becoming estranged and that she was considering a plan to make sure Miyuki would accept the role. With tomorrow's New Year's celebration in mind, she'd let Hayama in on her secret, delegating a variety of preparations to him.

"There were a few more complications than I'd expected, but that helped keep things lively. Now the only question is how cooperative Miyuki will be."

"I believe all will be well."

It was an uncharacteristically bold statement for him to make. On the sofa, Maya twisted around to look back at him curiously.

"Ms. Miyuki is far steadier and more able to face her own feelings than Master Tatsuya is. Master Tatsuya may be invincible in battle, but he is still no match for Ms. Miyuki's straightforward honesty."

"They say whoever loves more is the weaker, though."

Even Maya's cynicism was no match for the twinkle of Hayama's smile. "I believe in this case, madam, sincerity will carry the day."

When Tatsuya returned to their room, it was unoccupied. He supposed that Miyuki was somewhere else in the mansion getting some kind of spa treatment in preparation for tomorrow.

Just as Maya had said, notice that his bath was ready soon arrived. He rarely stayed the night at the mansion, and this was the first time he'd been given the Japanese-style guest room, so the bathing routine was unfamiliar to him. Going to and from the bath, he made sure to be dressed appropriately so that he wouldn't embarrass himself or anyone else. His bath wasn't especially long, nor did he rush. By the time he returned to his room, a glance at the clock revealed that it was nearly eleven, although his sister had yet to return.

Instead, the futon had been laid out.

A single futon set, for the single room. With two pillows.

And then, with the worst possible timing, Miyuki returned. "I'm sorry I'm late, Brother— Oh! They...!"

With the sliding door open, it was easy to see into the room. As soon as Miyuki entered, their eyes met.

"Miyuki, I didn't do—"

—*This*. But Tatsuya was unable to finish his apology. He took in the sight of Miyuki, in her simple single-layer kimono—which was nearly the same thing as seeing her in her underwear—having been polished to a shine by who knew how many servants. Having herself just emerged from the steamy bath, she didn't look the slightest bit cold, despite the midwinter chill. If anything, her face and neck appeared warm and flushed, though that was clearly not because of the room's temperature.

It wasn't seeing her in a thin kimono that had made Tatsuya fall silent. It was the uncharacteristically captivating allure that the kimono-clad girl was radiating that struck him.

Her beauty was always radiant, but in this moment, it seemed to be actually radiating.

She always had a certain pleasant, almost inorganic scent about her, but now the faintly floral fragrance that swirled about Miyuki seemed to draw him in, as though he were a bee to a flower.

If she were to walk around Tokyo like this, she would unquestionably cause disasters wherever she went, he thought.

But Miyuki was also flustered, and after freezing in her tracks at seeing the single futon laid out, she was the first one to speak. "Tatsuya, is this...?"

"I swear, I didn't lay it out like this. It was like this when I came back from the bath."

"I—I see..."

If they just stood there, they'd never clear the air, Tatsuya thought. He sat down in front of the room's low table and gestured for Miyuki to sit on a cushion. The idea of closing the sliding door that connected to the next room made him somehow uncomfortable, so he left it open.

Across from him, Miyuki, still agitated, fidgeted with her hair and collar. She seemed unusually conscious of his gaze on her.

There wasn't much he could do about that. It had only been three hours since the shock of their engagement—to say nothing of the bombshell that they weren't biological siblings. It would've been unfair to ask her not to be self-conscious.

"Um—T-Tatsuya..." Miyuki's voice was uncertain.

Tatsuya furrowed his brows in concern. "What's wrong?"

"Oh, um, it's just...can I still call you *Brother*? Or should I call you T...Ta..."

Miyuki couldn't get the rest of it out. Tatsuya smiled and threw her a line: "You can keep calling me what you always have."

Miyuki smiled in relief, but his answer hadn't just been for her. Tatsuya had no intention of internalizing the lie that she wasn't his sister.

"So then, Brother...did you and Aunt Maya finish your conversation?"

"Why else would I—" —*be here*, Tatsuya was about to answer, since it seemed obvious to him, but then he realized that the true meaning of Miyuki's question was something else. "Er, yes, we finished. She told me everything I needed to know about what's going on."

"I see. So then, um..." Miyuki fumbled for her words, but not out of uncertainty. She simply couldn't summon the nerve to ask the question. But eventually she wrung enough courage out of her heart to say it out loud. "Brother, about you and I not being biological siblings, is that—?"

—*Is that true?*

But no matter how much she tried, she couldn't get the last words out.

"It's a lie," Tatsuya stated simply.

And with those words, Miyuki's heart split in two.

One half was happy and relieved to be able to remain his sister, and the other half knew that as his sister, they could not marry.

"Why…? Why would Aunt Maya tell such a lie?"

"The explanation was hard to understand, but apparently she did it in order to allow us to marry."

It was true enough that Maya's explanation had been difficult to understand, but Tatsuya now had a grasp on the broader circumstances. But how much of that should he reveal to her? He still hadn't decided.

"Even though…we're siblings?"

"Evidently they're going to work something out with the DNA tests and family registers."

"I suppose…that the Yotsuba family does have enough influence to do that…"

"She also said that we don't have to worry about our children having any genetic abnormalities."

"How…could that be?" Miyuki had been looking down with a dark expression, but her eyes now came up to meet Tatsuya's. The collar of her clothing was slightly open and exposed a patch of enticingly pale skin, from which Tatsuya hastily averted his eyes. But such thoughts, he realized, played right into Maya's hand, so he strengthened his resolve.

His composure recovered, he looked again into Miyuki's eyes. Those eyes seemed ready to receive any truth he might speak.

Maya's decision to make Tatsuya Miyuki's companion in life was weighty enough to make Miyuki resolve to accept whatever came next.

Tatsuya saw that resolve in her eyes and solidified his determination to tell her what he knew he must.

"She said you have absolutely no genetic factors that could cause abnormality in your children.

"Because you were engineered."

Miyuki's eyes went wide, and she clasped her hands over her mouth.

Her long hair shook.

Her frightened face made her look her age. Even as he felt a bit relieved to see it, Tatsuya knew this was not the time for such thoughts.

"I'm...engineered...?"

"A fully engineered magician, created using the very best of the Yotsubas' science and magic, using a fertilized egg that came from our mother and father. A triumph over every flaw an engineered magician could have, something made by humans but greater than human. The greatest masterpiece of the Yotsuba family."

Tatsuya's explanation offered no comfort in the face of the fact that she was an engineered magician. And yet, somehow, Miyuki visibly regained her composure.

Her dismay and fear had not come from the revelation that she had been artificially created. Miyuki thought of her body and her self as having been bestowed upon her by Tatsuya. In fact, it was more accurate to say she assumed this was true beyond a doubt, so strong was her conviction.

"So then, I...I won't suddenly leave you and be cast into the abyss?"

What she *had* been afraid of was the unpredictable lifespan typical of engineered magicians. She was terrified that one day she would suddenly die and no longer be able to be with him.

"From the way Aunt Maya was talking, your capacity for continuous magic use is even higher than mine."

"So...I'll be able to have a life with you?"

"From the way Aunt Maya was talking, you'll probably outlive me."

Upon being told that she would live at least as long as her brother, Miyuki seemed not to care at all that she had been engineered. "So we're siblings...but my genes are different from yours, right?"

This was verging onto dangerous territory.

It was true that Maya had said that Miyuki's genetic code had been restructured, and she and Tatsuya were further apart, genetically, than Tatsuya and Maya—nephew and aunt—were. But Tatsuya hadn't breathed a word of that to Miyuki.

And yet, Miyuki was talking just like Maya had.

Tatsuya felt that there was more to blood relationships than genetic similarity.

"In any case, most of the Yotsuba family carries at least a few of the genetic modifications that came out of Lab Four. Even if they're not as complete as those done to engineered magicians, you and I are no different, inasmuch as we both carry genetic modifications."

Tatsuya tried to emphasize the similarity between them. But given Miyuki's flushed face, it didn't seem to be working.

"So from here on out, I'm going to be considered your cousin?" she asked.

"In front of other people, it seems so."

"And that'll mean I can be your fiancée!" Miyuki's voice rose with her emotions, but her excitement was not long-lived, because she then saw Tatsuya's troubled expression.

"You…think it's revolting, don't you…?"

"What is?" Tatsuya understood neither Miyuki's sudden dejection nor what she was saying in that sad, low tone.

"You still think of me as your little sister, don't you, Brother?"

"Yeah. I mean, that is factually accurate." Tatsuya was unwilling to budge on that point.

"And you think it's abnormal for a girl to want to be her biological brother's bride, don't you?"

"Miyuki, wait, you're not saying—" For a moment, Tatsuya thought he'd misheard. But thanks to his training, his five senses were far sharper than an ordinary person's.

Miyuki had unmistakably said *bride*. And meant *his*.

In other words, Miyuki wanted to…

"Yes, I am! It's not because Aunt Maya ordered it! When I heard that you were my betrothed, it made me so very happy!"

Miyuki's hands gripped her kimono as she looked down. Teardrops fell onto her hands and darkened her clothes. "And my feelings haven't changed. Even knowing that you *are* my real brother, I still want you to love me as a woman! I want to be your bride! I gave up on it once, so I can't give it up again!"

While Miyuki's voice was composed, her words were getting wound up.

But that phrasing. *I can't give it up again.* That meant that she'd agonized over this issue before today, which left Tatsuya thunderstruck. It was true that Miyuki frequently showed him more affection than most would consider usual. But Tatsuya had ultimately just thought that was making up for lost time given their history.

But now—as Miyuki's teardrops continued to fall—he was wondering if that was merely what he'd wanted to believe.

"But you're normal, Brother... You have good morals...so you'd never have romantic feelings for your sister, would you? It disgusts you to have a sister like me, I bet..." Miyuki began to sob.

She wasn't bawling or howling—it was the pitiful whimper of someone whose emotional dam had finally broken.

"Miyuki..." Tatsuya edged closer, reaching out to her shoulder.

Her hands came up to his.

Tatsuya was ready for her to brush his hand away. It would be no less than he deserved, he thought, for being so insensitive to her suffering and driving her to such wretched sobs.

But her hands closed over his and drew it to her chest.

"Hey—"

Tatsuya got halfway through saying "Hey, wait," and stopping her, but then stopped himself. He couldn't do anything that seemed in any way like he was pushing her away. No—he didn't want to.

"Brother, I...I..." Holding tightly to his hand, Miyuki forced the words out. "I'm in l-love with you. I love you. Brother, I'm in love with you!"

Tatsuya had heard his sister express affection for him many times. But this was the first time he had heard anything like this.

It was such a simple thing, but the weight of it was different. For the first time, he understood that.

"I don't even care if you hate your freak sister! I don't care if you think I'm sick! But...but please, please, Brother..." Miyuki looked up with a tear-streaked face.

Tatsuya had never seen anyone look so sad, so desperate, and so terribly beautiful.

"Just...just...please, don't send me away. Don't leave me. I'm begging you, don't ever leave me!"

Even while crying, Miyuki's face did not distort. Her features remained impeccably composed as the tears rolled down them. That was one more thing Tatsuya had realized for the first time today.

Her crying face was terribly sad, he thought.

Leaving his right hand where Miyuki held it, Tatsuya wrapped his left arm around Miyuki's back.

"Bro...ther...?"

"I will never leave you."

"Ah...er...would you say it again, please...?" Miyuki asked tremulously, burying her face in his chest and still clinging to his hand. She wanted to hear it again.

"Miyuki. I will never, ever leave you."

"Oh..." Miyuki sighed in an overwhelmed voice, and the strength seemed to go out of her body.

As Tatsuya lent Miyuki his body to lean against, he spoke the answer he had to speak.

"Until death parts us, I will always be by your side.

"But it may not be in the way you're hoping for.

"Right now, I can still only see you as my little sister.

"You're my dear little sister. I could never be disgusted by you.

"I don't think you're sick or a freak.

"I will never reject you. I will never push you away.

"But, Miyuki…that's because I am your brother. And you're my dear, sweet little sister.

"So…I'm sorry. But for now, anyway, I can only think of you as my sister."

Miyuki listened to Tatsuya, very still in his arms. When he was finished, she released the right hand she'd clung to and straightened.

"That's enough."

Miyuki's eyes were still moist. But no new tears were flowing.

"For now, that's enough for me." Miyuki softly put her arms around Tatsuya's neck and hugged him. "After all, I still can't bring myself to call you anything but *Brother*."

She put her cheek against his and whispered softly into his ear.

"And you said 'for now.' That's more than enough for me."

Miyuki squeezed Tatsuya more tightly. "Brother, is it all right if I look forward to it, though? Not soon, but someday…you seeing me not as your little sister, but as Miyuki."

"It might be a strange thing to say," he whispered into her ear, "but I'll try."

Miyuki released their embrace. "Gosh, Brother," she said with an exasperated chuckle.

Tatsuya smiled wryly. They'd finally regained their usual sibling mood. "Miyuki, it's late. Tomorrow's a big day, so we should sleep."

"Oh, you're right. I'll get another futon—"

Miyuki started to stand, but Tatsuya caught her.

"Brother?"

"There's no need. Aunt Maya went to all this trouble. We can sleep in the same futon tonight."

"Wha—?!" came Miyuki's shocked voice. Even when she'd been crying, she hadn't seemed this agitated. "E-er, Brother, do you mean that—?"

"Ah, no." Tatsuya flashed her a regretful smile. "I just mean sleeping side by side. There's multiple sheets."

"Oh…I see." Miyuki breathed a sigh of relief, but there was something in her manner that seemed just a bit disappointed—although perhaps that was reading too much into it.

"I'm going to change into sleeping clothes. Go ahead and get into the futon," said Tatsuya.

"No…I'll wait. Let's get in together."

"Okay. I'll be ready in a bit."

Tatsuya had already checked to make sure the room had *yukata* meant for sleeping in, so he didn't have to look around to find it. He quickly changed, leaving a pair of boxers on under the robe.

"Won't you be cold?" Miyuki asked as she turned down the comforter to make it easier for Tatsuya to sleep in.

"No, honestly with this I'll probably be too warm." Tatsuya laid down on the futon and beckoned Miyuki closer.

After just a moment's hesitation, she came close and laid her head on his arm.

"I wonder how long it's been. A long time ago, when we were really young, I seem to remember just once, you let me sleep in your arms like this."

"It wasn't that long ago… It was the night after Mom's funeral."

"That's…right. I can't believe I forgot that."

Miyuki snuggled closer.

Tatsuya wrapped his arms around her to draw her up against him.

"Brother…"

"What is it?"

"Did you not know at all?"

"Well…"

"How much I agonized over this?"

"Sorry."

"Especially recently. Magicians are expected to marry young. Once my position as a magician was settled, I'd prepared myself to have to immediately choose a fiancé, at the very least."

"I guess so."

"Siblings can't marry. So I thought it would have to be another man that I'd..."

"Miyuki." Tatsuya's hand stroked her hair soothingly. Miyuki flinched at first but soon relaxed, surrendering her body to Tatsuya. "Go to sleep."

"Yes, Brother..."

Miyuki entrusted both her body and heart to Tatsuya and drifted off to sleep, listening to the faint sound of a distant bell ringing in the New Year.

[7]

New Year's Day, 2097.

Tatsuya and Miyuki were both immediately, dizzyingly busy first thing in the morning.

They were quite used to rising early, so this was no great burden, but both of them were soon entirely fed up with being treated like Japanese-style dress-up dolls. Tatsuya obviously so, but even Miyuki, who knew how to put on a kimono by herself, was unaccustomed to having the whole process done by other people. When they seemed about to slather his face with makeup, Tatsuya drew a line and flatly refused, but Miyuki was not so lucky—although to be fair, she wasn't caked in makeup like a stage actor but merely given a *natural look for kimono fashion*-type makeover.

In any case, after having been fussed over for more than an hour, when they were finally released, the two were not at all inclined to go back to the house in their dolled-up states.

So they waited in a sitting room, in the rattan chairs they found there, trying not to wrinkle their outfits as they sought a moment's peace. Soon, though, Fumiya (wearing traditional *hakama* trousers) and Ayako (wearing a formal long-sleeved kimono) came to see them, having finished their own preparations.

"Tatsuya, Miyuki, many happy returns on the New Year," chorused the two with exquisite politeness. Miyuki and Tatsuya stood to greet them.

"Fumiya, Ayako, happy New Year. Oh, wait, are we still on a first-name basis today?"

"Don't start the New Year by teasing us, Tatsuya. It's fine. I'll make an exception for you, so you still get to call me Ayako."

Miyuki giggled. "Fumiya, Ayako—Happy New Year!"

"Whoa…" Fumiya murmured. "Miyuki…how do I put this? You look very beautiful."

"Are you serious? She just looks like herself." Ayako sounded exasperated but didn't seem sincerely antagonized—given that today was all about Miyuki, she'd already accepted that there would be a certain difference in how they were treated.

"But anyway, Miyuki, that's an absolutely *stunning* kimono. You practically look like a bride!"

This appraisal had occurred to Miyuki herself, so all she could do was smile a bit awkwardly at the compliment. "I tried to tell them it was too much, but…they insisted that it had been set aside for me to wear today."

"My goodness." It was hard to tell whether the tone of Ayako's voice was sympathetic surprise or envy.

"I imagine that Mrs. Shirakawa considers the naming of the successor to be an occasion worthy of formality," a new voice cut in. It was Yuuka—also wearing a formal kimono.

"Happy New Year, Yuuka. Thank you again for your help yesterday," said Tatsuya.

"Happy New Year, Tatsuya. And you're very welcome. Please don't worry about it," said Yuuka as she amiably joined the four.

After everyone exchanged the proper pleasantries, Yuuka suggested that they sit.

With five people now occupying it, the sitting room had begun to feel a bit small. This made it that much easier to notice certain conspicuous absences.

It was Fumiya who broached the topic—he was the youngest, after all. "I wonder if Mr. Shibata will be attending."

"There's not much time left; I suppose he might be let directly into the event. Or possibly, he'll attend with his parents," Tatsuya offered.

The clock on the wall let everyone see that they'd soon be called for the formalities to begin. Then as though to reinforce Tatsuya's supposition, a housekeeper wearing a formal kimono in muted colors came to the sitting room to summon them.

"Pardon me for interrupting. My name is Minami Sakurai, and I have the honor of showing you to today's event." Today, Minami's role as guide involved explaining why she was wearing a formal kimono, despite being house staff. "I apologize in advance for any insufficiency, and I will do my very best to serve in this capacity."

True to her words, she seemed quite nervous. Acting as a guide for the New Year's celebration diverged quite a bit from her normal duties, and there were parts of it that she suspected were being performed incorrectly due to anachronistic misinterpretation of traditional culture, which she found a little embarrassing.

"Fumiya, sir, Ayako, miss, allow me to guide you first."

Fumiya and Ayako nodded to Tatsuya, Miyuki, and Yuuka to take their leave, then stood.

The two fell in stride behind Minami as they quietly followed her out of the sitting room.

"That reminds me, Tatsuya—do you know how arriving at the New Year's celebration works?"

Tatsuya thought it was a bit late to be asking that question, but he answered honestly. "The guide calls for you, and then you're walked to the venue."

Yuuka regarded Tatsuya pityingly. "So I assume, Miyuki...?"

"Yes. That is also what I have heard."

"I see... Well, let me give you a piece of advice."

Tatsuya and Miyuki shared a dubious glance, then looked back to Yuuka.

Completely serious and straight-faced, Yuuka continued. "When you walk in, you *cannot* laugh. If you don't think you can take it, try to just sit down and bow. It's a Japanese-style room, so that way you can hide it if you start to crack up."

After Yuuka left for the hall, a few minutes passed.

Minami returned to the sitting room and informed Tatsuya and Miyuki that their turn had arrived. "Tatsuya, sir, Miyuki, miss. Allow me to guide you."

"...Minami, are you okay? You seem kind of tired."

True to Miyuki's question, Minami did seem exhausted.

"No, I am fine. My apologies, but if we could be brisk—"

Perhaps after her duties as guide were complete, she would be allowed to rest, Tatsuya mused. He urged Miyuki along, hoping that speeding things up would make Minami's life a little easier.

"Presenting a candidate for succession to family head, Ms. Miyuki Shiba, escorted by her elder brother, Mr. Tatsuya Shiba."

Minami's pompous announcement almost made Tatsuya fall right over. He glanced over at Miyuki and saw her cheek twitching as she fought to contain a giggle. If not for Yuuka's warning, there was no question that both of them would've disgraced themselves.

The assembled house staff all prostrated themselves, making it that much harder for both Tatsuya and Miyuki to maintain their composure.

Nevertheless, both siblings managed to retain a distinguished carriage as they bowed at the waist in return, Tatsuya dignified and Miyuki graceful.

Is this some kind of test to see how long we can keep a straight face? Tatsuya wondered to himself as he bowed.

Minami came alongside the pair. "Allow me to show you to your seats," she murmured.

Tatsuya and Miyuki took this as their signal to look up.

There immediately rose a murmur from the assembled attendees—clearly the effect of Miyuki's appearance.

Led by Minami, the Shiba siblings took their seats.

There was another murmur.

The siblings had been seated directly next to Maya.

"Welcome, everyone, and again, many happy returns on the New Year," Maya began, bringing the murmur to a sharp stop. Despite being unmarried, she wore a formal black kimono liberally embroidered in gold.

After a beat, there was a religious chorus of "Happy New Year!" from the guests. Tatsuya and Miyuki had anticipated this, so they managed not to be late in adding their voices.

Maya looked around the room, seeming satisfied. "In addition to celebrating the beginning of an auspicious New Year, I am delighted to say that I have three pieces of wonderful news to share with you all today."

With that preamble, Maya first looked to Katsushige. Sitting next to Katsushige—who like Tatsuya was wearing *hakama* trousers and a *haori* jacket—was a very awkward-looking Kotona, who like Miyuki wore a formal kimono.

"I'd like to take this opportunity to announce the engagement of Mr. Katsushige Shibata, the eldest son of the Shibata family, to Ms. Kotona Tsutsumi."

A ripple of murmurs spread through the room. To Tatsuya's ear, the "Finally!" and "I knew it" reactions seemed to outnumber the "Surely not!" ones.

"While I'm sure that the future holds both joy and hardship alike for them, I ask that you join me in wishing this young couple the very best of luck."

Applause rose in the room. But before it did, Tatsuya didn't miss the fact that a majority of people seemed to nod when Maya mentioned *hardship*.

"Next, I'd like to turn to a matter about which I know you all are deeply concerned."

Silence fell upon the assembled as though they'd been doused in cold water.

Maya chuckled. "I see you all know what I'm talking about."

Silence persisted—there was not so much as a whisper in the room.

With a smile that betrayed nothing of what she might really be thinking, Maya announced the name of the next head of the Yotsuba family. "My successor will be Ms. Miyuki Shiba."

After a breath's pause, there was a wave of energetic applause—the bulk of which came from the domestic staff of the main house.

"We'll leave her introductions for another time. A New Year's celebration is no occasion for such stuffy formalities, after all."

This was met with a scatter of approving laughter. From what Tatsuya could see, most of the voices belonged to men whose faces seemed flushed. This clearly wasn't a dry event, he realized with some surprise.

"And now, my final announcement. I would like to announce the engagement of my successor, Ms. Miyuki Shiba, to my son, Mr. Tatsuya Shiba."

Instead of applause, a stir of commotion swept over the room. People were no longer just whispering to one another.

"Excuse me, madam. Might I be permitted a question?"

The voice came from beside Yuuka. It belonged to a woman wearing a black kimono with muted colors—it was Yuuka's mother, the head of the Tsukuba family, Touka Tsukuba.

"Certainly, Mrs. Tsukuba. What is it?" replied Maya with an unconcerned, serene smile.

Touka continued with a stiff face that was anything but unconcerned. "Just now you used the words *my son*, but perhaps I misheard. To my recollection, Tatsuya is the son of your late sister, Miya."

"Indeed. So let me take this opportunity to introduce my son. Tatsuya Shiba, who sits right here, is my son, conceived from an egg I donated before the incident, with my late sister Miya acting as a surrogate mother and carrying him. As such, he was given to her to raise, but as of tonight, I have decided to receive him as my son."

The murmurs fell silent—but just for a moment.

"Madam—"

"Ah, Mitsugu. Whatever might you have to say?" Given the occasion, the main family head ought to have addressed a branch family head more formally, as *Mr. Kuroba*, but Maya had called him simply *Mitsugu*. She was well aware that this would only increase the pressure on him.

"Just now you said *receive*, but—"

"Ah, yes, I see. I suppose my wording does invite a misunderstanding." In sharp contrast to his strained features, Maya's expression was so airily blithe she seemed about to chuckle. "As Tatsuya is still in his second year of schooling at First High, he will continue to live at the Shiba house. Normally there would be some cause for moral concern given two engaged high school students living together, but I have faith that Miyuki and Tatsuya will not allow anything untoward to happen."

"But—" Just as he was about to protest further, Mitsugu stopped.

He finally realized that beside him, Fumiya was repeatedly whispering, "Sis, are you okay?"

"My goodness, Ayako. Are you all right? Do you feel unwell?" Maya asked, before Mitsugu could say anything.

Guilt over his daughter froze Mitsugu in his tracks.

"No…I'm…all right," said Ayako firmly, although anyone could see that she was anything but all right.

"Would someone please help Ayako to another room?" asked Maya, a request that Fumiya and Minami immediately answered.

At the entrance to the large room, Minami prostrated herself. "I will guide her, madam," she said.

"Here, lean on me," Fumiya said, putting his arm around Ayako's shoulders and looking to Maya questioningly.

"Yes, if you would," said Maya to Minami, then turned to Fumiya. "Fumiya, you may be excused."

As Ayako lay in bed, having changed from her formal kimono into more comfortable clothing, there was a knock at her door.

"Sis, I'm coming in."

It was Minami, who'd accompanied Ayako into the room, who opened the door from the inside.

"Oh, Fumiya." Ayako started to sit up in bed, at which Fumiya rushed to her side and drew the bedclothes back up.

"No, Sis, c'mon! You have to sleep!"

"You're making such a fuss. It's not like I'm sick," grumbled Ayako. Nevertheless, she did lie back down.

At this protest, Fumiya looked away, but then he soon put on a brave face and looked her in the eye. "Sis, look…are you okay?"

"Geez…I guess you can tell, can't you, Fumiya?" Ayako smiled, though her expression was on the verge of tears. "Maybe it's because we're twins. Y'know, in times like this, it's a real pain not being able to hide anything from you."

Fumiya's expression seemed to mirror Ayako's. There was no way anyone would mistake the two as identical, but as they both smiled and tried to hold back tears, their matching expressions made them seem very much a pair.

"…You went up against Miyuki, so what could you do? She's closer to Tatsuya than anyone else." *So you'll have to give up on Tatsuya*—but he left that part unsaid. His statement all but said her crush on Tatsuya was a given, and Ayako raised no words of denial.

"Still, I can't believe the family head would go so far to take Miyuki's side…"

"That's not it, Fumiya." Fumiya had understood Maya's theatrics in taking Tatsuya as her own son to be for Miyuki's benefit. But Ayako immediately disagreed. "This is for Tatsuya's sake."

"Sis?"

"This isn't for Miyuki. Maya used Miyuki in order to guarantee *Tatsuya's* position and freedom."

"I suppose…"

Fumiya took her claim as bravado in service of self-protection—to avoid thinking that Miyuki had been chosen as Tatsuya's bride because she was the most suitable girl.

It never occurred to him that Ayako had in fact cut to the very heart of the matter.

Thanks to the disruption caused by Ayako's fainting, the matter of the shocking announcement that Tatsuya was Maya's biological son was only vaguely resolved—and without any of the obvious follow-up questions like *Is that true?* or *If it is true, why was it hidden until now?* However, that meant within that vague resolution, Tatsuya's position as Maya's son and Miyuki's betrothed was established.

But that didn't mean that someone who so much of the family had reviled as a misbegotten failure would suddenly be respected now that he was the family head's son and the intended of her successor. No matter how many ruffled feathers were smoothed, disdain still tinted their every word and action.

Tatsuya didn't blame them for this, though. For one thing, he was sitting at a banquet table, but more than anything else, as the central figure in all of this, he was fully aware of the farce at its heart. If anything, he felt sympathetic toward the family members and household staff who now suddenly had to change their overt attitude to him.

However, there were those who were incapable of overlooking the staff's unbecoming attitudes.

Wearing a morning coat, Hayama approached Maya—which meant he also approached Tatsuya and Miyuki—and prostrated himself.

"Tatsuya, sir, Miyuki, miss—allow me to offer my congratulations."

"Thank you so much," Miyuki gracefully replied.

"Thank you—but please, look up," Tatsuya said, uncomfortable with such grandiose gestures. "I don't know the first thing about the work and conventions of the main house. I know I'll need you to teach me all about it." It was an ad hoc attempt, but Tatsuya did an admirable job of attempting to cut the awkward interaction short.

But Hayama had no intention of letting the little drama end so easily. "I would be honored. Please ask this old butler anything at all. By the way, sir, do you happen to remember?"

Not having attended the drama's script meeting, Tatsuya didn't have the faintest clue. But there was no need for him to go digging through his memory, as Hayama quickly provided the answer.

"I seem to recall that you promised to demonstrate some new magic at this year's celebration," said Hayama.

"New magic? Tatsuya, does that mean you've finished it?" Maya looked at him with such hungry curiosity that it was clear she wasn't just playing along. Of course she wasn't.

"—Yes," said Tatsuya carefully, successfully course-correcting from the noncommittal *Uh, sure* that would've been his usual answer. Given his current condition, he had no inclination whatsoever to disparage the household staff.

"Really?! Oh, I'd simply love to see it!" Maya chimed in with girlish glee.

Tatsuya gave Hayama a glare with all the resentment he could muster, but the old butler merely took in Maya's suddenly youthful demeanor with a beatific, grandfatherly smile.

For some reason, even Miyuki was piling on the fray. "Brother—er, Tatsuya, that is. May I watch, too?"

He was completely surrounded. There was no longer room for him to refuse.

"All right. I'll need to do some preparation, so if you'll excuse me."

Still wearing his *hakama* trousers and *haori* jacket, Tatsuya reappeared in the garden adjoining the meeting hall, carrying his CAD case.

At the opposite end of the garden was a cage containing a wild boar.

Tatsuya turned to face the seats in the meeting hall and began his explanation in a loud, clear voice.

"The novel magic Baryon Lance is a lethal spell for use against biological targets. This demonstration will therefore be somewhat bloody. I suggest that anyone who prefers not to witness pointless killing go wait in a separate room."

Quite a few people looked to their neighbors upon hearing this warning, but none left their seats. Tatsuya supposed that meant everyone here was related to the Yotsuba.

"In that case, I'll begin."

Even as he wondered why he had to participate in this absurd carnival show, he opened the case and took out his improved custom Silver Horn, Trident.

He normally wielded Trident as part of a pair in a dual-gun style, but today he held it by itself in his right hand, affixing a bayonet-like attachment to the barrel. It was quite long and gave the gun an overall rather unbalanced appearance.

Tatsuya pointed the bayonet at the boar in the cage.

Without any fanfare, he pulled the trigger.

The magical processes all fired in an instant.

Material: Baryon Decomposition
The atomic nuclei in the bayonet are decomposed by first separating its

molecules into atoms, then its atoms into electrons and nuclei, then splitting
its nuclei into baryons like protons and neutrons.

FAE Process Execution: Particle Concentration

Per FAE theory, with the particles now free from the constrains of
physical laws, instead of scattering as those laws would dictate, they are
concentrated into a thin disk shape. The leptons—electrons—not targeted
by the decomposition are captured by protons.

FAE Process Execution: Ejection

The concentrated disk of baryons is fired at the target. Traveling accord-
ing to FAE theory, the disk reaches speeds of ten thousand kilometers per
second, exceeding the limits of magical force.

Material: Regeneration

All processes are reversed.

Voices rose from the assembled guests as the boar fell to the
ground with a loud thud.

"Huh?"

"What?"

"What happened?"

Tatsuya was not so service oriented that he was inclined to deliver
a detailed explanation. He gave a brief bow to the assembled staff and
members of the clan and was about to pack his CAD and its bayonet
attachment (which itself was a variety of CAD) back into its case.

But then, unfortunately, a voice stopped him short.

"Wait a moment."

It was Katsushige.

"Yes?" Tatsuya asked in a neutral tone.

Katsushige descended into the garden wearing wooden geta san-
dals. He approached the caged boar and looked carefully at its dead
body.

"That was a high-density neutron beam, wasn't it? The boar's tissues are boiling. For some reason, the cells aren't radioactive, so how is it that you're managing to produce this effect?"

"The 'how' is secret." Tatsuya didn't think Katsushige was actually asking for him to share a magic technique, but he shut down the attempt just in case.

"Obviously," Katsushige shot back.

Tatsuya ignored the barb. "But I suppose I can explain what just transpired. That shouldn't be too difficult." He showed his Trident, the bayonet still attached to it, to Katsushige. "This weapon is a CAD with a single activation program and a carbon steel spike."

True to Tatsuya's description, upon closer inspection, the bayonet attachment was more of a spike than a blade.

"The spike is decomposed to the baryon level, concentrated into a disk, and shot at the target."

The firing process used the same FAE—Free After Execution—theory that Angelina Sirius's Brionac used, but Tatsuya had absolutely no intention of revealing that here.

"So it wasn't an optical illusion that I saw the spike portion disappear for a moment. I see." Katsushige was satisfied for a moment but soon continued his interrogation. "So the weapon is decomposed into protons and neutrons? What about the electrons? ...Oh, I see. The protons become neutrons via electron capture. That's why it's a neutron beam, not a charged particle beam... So why is the spike still there after it's been fired?"

Tatsuya was inwardly mystified as to why Katsushige was being so persistent in his questioning, but he decided there was no harm in answering the question. "I regenerated it."

"Ah! Of course, I see!"

"Oh! I see it now!" Maya's voice rang out through the garden, overlapping Katsushige's frustrated exclamation. "*That's* why it's called Baryon *Lance*—not *cannon* or *launcher* or even *gun*, but *lance*—because the final step uses regeneration magic."

From Tatsuya's perspective, he'd explained enough for that to be obvious, but either way, what Maya said was correct, so he faced her and gave her a crisp bow.

"And the fact that there's no radioactive material left over is because by using regeneration, the neutrons you just fired are all retrieved. The attack's only effect is the neutron beam superheating the water in the target's body. Tatsuya, it's splendid!"

Tatsuya bowed again.

As his head was lowered, Katsushige spoke to him in a low murmur, such that nobody else could hear. "Couldn't you have used that magic to beat us easily?"

Tatsuya now understood all his persistent questions. But *this* question had missed the point entirely, and Tatsuya was merciless in his response.

"Baryon Lance is designed to eliminate targets that Dismantle won't work on. There would be no reason to use it with opponents susceptible to Dismantle."

Katsushige, red-faced, fell silent. He clearly understood the implied message—*If I'd used Dismantle, it would've been over immediately.*

Katsushige gave Tatsuya a keen-eyed stare. But he did nothing foolish or violent that would've endangered himself, the Shibata family, or Kotona. He calmed his breathing, pushed his mortification down into his heart, schooled his expression of surprise at this new magic technique, and returned to his seat.

With this, the demonstration was over. Tatsuya kept his guard up for anyone who might come and pester him with questions about a "neutron barrier," but no such boors appeared.

Perhaps the fact that they were at a celebratory dinner was acting as a kind of social barrier.

If "neutron barriers" had come up, then he would've had to reveal another part of the secret, so Tatsuya was relieved it hadn't.

There were no further incidents at the New Year's celebration. Little by little, Tatsuya was rewritten as the son of the Yotsuba family head, Maya Yotsuba, and was officially engaged to his sister.

The next day was January 2, 2097. A notice went out from the Yotsuba family through the Magic Association of Japan to the Ten Master Clans, the Eighteen Support Clans, the Hundred Families, and the rest of the Numbers. It informed them—

That Miyuki Shiba had been named as the successor to the Yotsuba family.

That Tatsuya Shiba had been acknowledged as Maya Yotsuba's son but that his name would remain Tatsuya Shiba.

That Miyuki Shiba and Tatsuya Shiba were engaged.

Within the day, the Yotsuba family's private message box at the Magic Association of Japan soon filled with messages of congratulations.

But not all of the Numbers sent well-wishes.

A day later, on January 3, 2097, an official protest was lodged with the Magic Association of Japan against the betrothal of Tatsuya Shiba and Miyuki Shiba.

The name on the protest was Gouki Ichijou, the current head of the Ichijou family, of the Ten Master Clans.

(To be continued in the Master Clans Conference arc)

AFTERWORD

Did you enjoy Volume 16, the Yotsuba Succession arc of *The Irregular at Magic High School*? This Yotsuba Succession arc is a turning point for the series, and beginning with the next volume, the story will be going in a new direction. It might have seemed like *Irregular* was heading toward its conclusion, but things aren't going to wrap up that easily, as I imagine you can tell from the final sentences—which weren't very "final" at all.

In this volume, I introduced some new characters who are either in college or beginning their professional careers. Because this story has a magic high school for its setting half the time, there hasn't been much opportunity for the non–high school students to show their stuff—alumni functions notwithstanding. So here in the afterword, I'd like to touch on some of these new characters.

First, Yuuka Tsukuba. She's five foot three and is a bit underweight at 105 pounds. She's twenty-two years old and is a senior at the Magic University. When she attended First High, she was the vice president of the student council, coming in just as Mayumi's generation was on their way out. Her straight hair is cropped to shoulder length and parted on the right. Her ears are pierced. As a magician, she specializes in mental interference magic.

Next we have Katsushige Shibata. He's six foot two and weighs 175 pounds. He keeps his straight hair cut in a short, professional cut. He's twenty-three years old and, since graduation from the Magic University, works for the Ministry of Defense. He does administrative work but possesses the combat magic abilities one would expect a man of his build to have. He specializes in the convergent magic discipline of density manipulation and by normal metrics is an excellent magician.

Third is Kotona Tsutsumi. She's five foot three and weighs 125 pounds. Her chestnut-brown hair is medium long and set in loose, soft curls. She's twenty-four years old and at a glance looks sort of like a "popular girl" type. In her professional life, she works as Katsushige's Guardian. She is one of the second-generation Bard series of engineered magicians and possesses a high facility for sound-manipulation magic.

Finally, there's Kanata Tsutsumi. He's five foot seven and 135 pounds, with shaggy chestnut hair. At twenty years old, he's a junior at the Magic University. He's also a semiprofessional musician who plays live shows regularly, but his main job is as Katsushige's Guardian. He's Kotona's biological younger brother, and like her, he specializes in sound-manipulation magic.

Each of these characters has more side stories to them than I could possibly fit here, but it is undetermined whether they'll ever be properly told.

Thank you all again for following this story for so long. The next volume will see a return to magic high school as the main setting.

What will be the repercussions of the Yotsuba succession among Tatsuya's and Miyuki's classmates and friends? And what will be the leading ten families' next move?

The next volume, 17, will be part one of the Master Clans Conference arc. I hope you'll look forward to it.

Tsutomu Sato

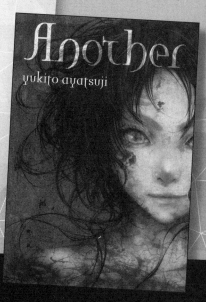

THE Eminence IN Shadow

ONE BIG FAT LIE
AND A FEW TWISTED TRUTHS

Even in his past life, Cid's dream wasn't to become a protagonist or a final boss. He'd rather lie low as a minor character until it's prime time to reveal he's a mastermind...or at least, do the next best thing—pretend to be one! And now that he's been reborn into another world, he's ready to set the perfect conditions to live out his dreams to the fullest. Cid jokingly recruits members to his organization and makes up a whole backstory about an evil cult that they need to take down. Well, as luck would have it, these imaginary adversaries turn out to be the real deal—and everyone knows the truth but him!

 For more information
visit www.yenpress.com

IN STORES NOW!

KAGE NO JITSURYOKUSHA NI NARITAKUTE !
©Daisuke Aizawa 2018 Illustration: Touzai / KADOKAWA CORPORATION